The Pulptress VS. THE BONE QUEEN

BLOOD AND BONE

ANDREA JUDY

PRO SE PRESS

PRO SE ⚖ PRESS

THE PULPTRESS VS. THE BONE QUEEN:
BLOOD AND BONE
A Pro Se Press Publication

This story is fictional. All of the characters in this publication are fictitious and any resemblance to actual persons, living or dead is purely coincidental. No part of this publication may be reproduced or transmitted in any form or by any means, graphic, electronic, or mechanical, including photocopying, recording, taping, or by any information storage or retrieval system, without the permission in writing of the publisher.

Edited by Tommy Hancock and Morgan McKay
Editor in Chief, Pro Se Productions—Tommy Hancock
Submissions Editor—Barry Reese
Director of Corporate Operations—Morgan McKay
Publisher & Pro Se Productions, LLC Chief Executive Officer—Fuller Bumpers

Cover art by Jeff Hayes
Print production and book design by Forrest Dylan Bryant
E-book design by Russ Anderson
New Pulp logo design by Sean E. Ali
New Pulp seal design by Cari Reese

Pro Se Productions, LLC
133 1/2 Broad Street
Batesville, AR 72501
870-834-4022

editorinchief@prose-press.com
www.prose-press.com

THE PULPTRESS VS. THE BONE QUEEN ©2015 Andrea Judy

BLOOD AND BONE

 Prologue

T HE PALE SKINNED WOMAN waited in her seat as everyone around her began rushing to grab their bags and disembark from the plane. She tugged at the ends of the baggy sweater she wore, and pulled her hair over her face again before glancing over her shoulder at her equally pale companion.

The man nodded absently, murmuring, "Soon."

Once the crowds began to thin, he pulled out her wheelchair, and put a hand to her hips, supporting her as she sat herself in the chair. He draped a black blanket carefully over her chest and down her legs. He pulled their only carry-on item, a long thin case from the overhead compartment and placed it in her lap before beginning to wheel her off the plane.

The flight attendant rushed over. "Do y'all need any help?" She asked.

He quickly shook his head. "No," he said flatly, and pushed the wheelchair past her.

The Bone Queen sneered, and didn't respond as she and her companion reached the Atlanta airport rolling past the gates and throngs of people that gathered around the baggage carrousel. He steered her through the crowds, trying to avoid most of them as he tried to guide them to car rental counter.

She kept her hand on the end of her bag. The gemstone of her sword handle vibrated subtly against her hand, speaking to her, telling her that what she searched for was closer, but still not within grasp.

"Get us a vehicle, Eten," she directed the man wheeling her around.

He nodded and stirred the wheelchair to the car rental area of the airport.

"Can I help you?" The woman at the counter said.

Eten cleared his throat and handed her a fake driver's license. "I need to rent a car."

She smiled, and took his license, and pulled out the stack of paperwork. The woman behind the counter went over the rules and regulations behind renting a car, but Eten's gaze lingered on the woman in the chair.

"Sir, your signature." The clerk said.

Eten nodded, signing everything and collecting the keys.

"Have a peachy stay in Georgia!" The clerk said with a smile.

The woman in the chair grunted as Eten wheeled her out to the lot where a sleek black car waited for them.

Lifting the chair up, she shoved it into the trunk of the car before seating herself in the passenger side with her sword in her lap. Eten got into the driver's side and started up the car. It jerked awkwardly as he slowly sorted out which pedal did what and how to best maneuver the car. He absently rubbed at his elbow where he could feel his skin starting to peel away.

"Where to?" he asked, glancing toward her.

She pulled the blanket off of her legs and stretched. The bones of her rib cage exposed to the warmth of the sun. She glanced at Eten and then to the sword. She held her hand over it for a few moments before pointing, "North."

He nodded and, as always, blindly obeyed.

They traveled for several hours in total silence. She occasionally pointed a different direction, and Eten served as dutiful chauffeur. The stars had taken over the sky by the time they passed the Epsilon, Georgia sign.

She sat up straighter, "Here. Turn." She said.

Eten led the car down a dirt road and past a cemetery, and then off of the road through grass and trees. He only stopped when she held up her hand.

Without another word, she got out of the car and began walking across the wooded area. Eten sat behind the steering wheel watching her. He glanced back toward the road, knowing there was nowhere he could hide from her. He took a deep, unnecessary breath before getting out of the car and following behind her.

She walked through the woods with her sword in her hand, weaving through the trees with ease, letting only the stone and the dull light of the moon guide her.

She finally paused and pointed toward what looked like a rundown old church. "Here is where we start," she said, using her sword to easily pry the door open and step into the long abandoned room.

She walked in slow deliberate steps before finding what she wanted: the entry to the crypt.

A slow, wicked smile curved her face as she descended the stairs. A chill shook through Eten's long dead body as he followed behind her and watched her begin to dig into the corpses she found in the crypt.

Time had long disintegrated everything but bones in

heaps against the crypt floor. She grabbed a rib cage and broke off a tip of bone before popping it into her mouth like candy. The bones slid past her lips and clattered out of her broken, exposed rib cage. She ate bite after bite, moving from body to body and devouring.

As each bone landed a small cloud of dust rose, and from the dust stepped a shambling body. Skin pulled too tight across long dead bones; their eyes saw nothing, and their mouths hung limply open. They shuffled after her, dragging their feet, and waiting her instructions.

Eten stayed back, looking away from the corpses that were too close to being like him. At least he still had his mind, and wasn't one of those mindless things. She'd been that kind to him.

She turned to the dozen or so corpses she had brought back. "My chiffoniers," she said, almost fondly, "Dig tunnels and search through this cemetery. Bring me the bones of the dead, and find me the stones that look like this." She pointed to the hilt of her sword. "Go."

The corpses nodded, obeying the tasks laid before them. They scrambled through the crypt to begin their slow work of cutting through the dirt and searching the fields. Eten watched them go until she touched his shoulder.

"Come, Eten. We must prepare my chambers and ready for her." She spat the last word.

Eten's brows furrowed, his decayed mind confused. "Her?" He asked.

The Bone Queen narrowed her eyes and ran her hand over the chipped rib in her chest. "The Pulptress."

1

W HEN I GOT A call at three in the morning, the last
thing I expected to hear on the line was an unfamiliar
voice telling me, "I found your name and number in
the hand of a dead man who just came back to life."

I nearly dropped the phone, staring at the ceiling in
stunned silence for several long seconds. "Who is this?"
I finally asked when my mouth could form words again.

"My name is Jackson," the woman's voice answered. "I'm
a coroner with the Epsilon Police Department."

"And how did you get this number?" I asked again trying
to think who this could really be, what kind of a set-up
this really was.

The woman on the line sighed heavily. "There's a dead
man who came back to life, and he had your name and this
phone number clutched in his hand. I don't know what it
means but—"

"Where are you?" I demanded as I rolled out of my bed
in the middle of Atlanta, GA.

I tossed off my pajamas and pulled on a pair of jeans and
a t-shirt, better to look like a disheveled college student
than stick out if this was a set up. I never unpacked when I

got to this little hotel yesterday. Looks like the leads about the dead coming to life that I'd been chasing down might have found me instead.

There was only one thing I'd ever met that made dead things come back to life, and if that corpse of a woman who had turned my life upside down in Paris nearly a year ago was back trap or not, I wasn't going to miss the chance to finish her off for good. She'd taken one of my mentors, one of my only friends, killed him and then brought him back to life just to fight me. If that woman calling herself the Bone Queen was back, then I had Amaury to avenge.

"Epsilon, Georgia." Jackson replied, rattling off an address that I hastily copied onto a coffee-stained napkin on my bedside table.

"Where is that?" I asked around the pen in my mouth. I grabbed my bag of guns and checked over my equipment. Guns, knives, ammo, batons, and a wide range of clothes were still safely packed away in two bags. The Body Box, my personal disappearing trick sat on the bathroom counter still.

Walking over to it, I easily chose a simple disguise, blonde hair, bags under my eyes, and pink lipstick, exhausted college freshmen. The Body Box let me be anyone to anyone so no one knew who they had even been dealing with.

Jackson chuckled faintly, and I got the distinct impression she answered that question on a regular basis. "It's in the middle of nowhere basically. If you see a Wal-Mart you've gone too far," she said. "It's off the 318. If you've got a GPS, it'll get you here, just might take you down a couple dirt roads."

I nodded absently as I threw the Body Box into a bag with my clothes. "I'll be there before morning."

"I'll have a pot of coffee waiting," Jackson promised

before hanging up.

I grabbed my things, and hurried out to my car, shoving everything into the trunk, before hopping into the driver's seat and carefully putting in the address Jackson had just given me. Estimated time to arrival: three hours. Peeling out of the parking lot, I tore off into the night, ready to finally catch the woman who killed Amaury.

After hitting the first dirt road, I realized that Jackson hadn't been joking about being in the middle of nowhere. The road was cleared but the dirt and gravel laid uneven and my car jumped and jerked.

I finally found a solid road again and slowed down, counting out house numbers until I pulled up in front of the address Jackson had given me.

The sun had just started to rise and cast the little building in an eerie pink-gold light that made the vinyl siding look like flames swallowed the structure whole. It looked like a simple house, though a sign in front of it labeled it as part of the Epsilon Police Department. A single beat up, rusted pickup truck with the license plate 'DRBONES1' sat in the driveway.

I cleared my throat, and checked my firearm carefully tucked into the pocket of my Georgia State hoodie before I walked straight up to the front door and knocked three times. Lost college student disguise was ready to go.

After a few moments, a young woman opened the door. Freckles dotted across her dark brown skin, and her curly black hair was pushed back behind a hot rod red headband with a large rose just behind her left ear.

The woman looked me over before grinning, "I didn't think you'd be blonde." She finally said.

I shifted faintly on my feet, "Jackson?" I asked.

She nodded, "So I'm guessing you might be this

Pulptress person?" She said as she offered her hand.

Her hands felt clammy and cold against my palm, and as soon as she let go, I wiped them on my jeans.

"Sorry," Jackson offered. "Sweaty palms when I'm nervous."

"So what happened?" I asked, stepping into the entryway.

Pale tile lined the floor and old wood paneling coated the walls. An empty desk sat at the front with a note that read 'Please ring the bell for service.' I had the distinct impression that no one came here to ring the bell for service.

"Just like I told you on the phone." Jackson collected a clipboard from the desk. "I was about to start doing an autopsy on a John Doe, and the next thing I know he's sitting up."

"You said he had my name and number in his hand?"

Jackson nodded, "Yeah, I didn't notice that until I uh… knocked him back down."

"Until you what?" I asked, frowning as I peered over her shoulder to look at file in her hand. Nothing useful there. Just listing a John Doe roughly 30 years old with blonde hair.

"I hit him," Jackson said. "He startled me and I just… POW. Right in the kisser."

"And what did he do?" I asked, glancing down at her hand. Her left knuckles were bruised with bits of blood on them; she'd recently punched something hard no doubt.

"Well he went back down. I tied him up, and that was when I noticed the note in his hand."

I paused and stared at her, "Are you saying that he's still here?" I asked, trying to keep my mouth from hanging open.

"Well I tied him up and put him back in the freezer," Jackson elaborated at my shocked face. "I didn't know what to do! Bodies don't get up and come after me on a real regular basis!"

"So you tied up a living dead and put him in the freezer?" I repeated back to her. I'd done and seen some wild things in my life, but that was a new one.

"Well what was I supposed to do?" She protested, "This doesn't happen here!"

"Just take me to wherever you have it," I finally said, pulling out my pistol from my hoodie pocket and carefully loading it.

"You are not shooting that in my lab!" Jackson shook her head, "Absolutely not!"

I sighed. "I'm a good enough shot I won't hit anything important, but fine." Reluctantly I put the gun away and pulled out a knife from the holster hidden under my hoodie. "Lead the way."

Jackson finally relented, moving through the house, wringing her thin hands together as she unlocked a basement door and started down the narrow, but well-lit stairs. She unlocked another door that opened into a solid white room with no windows. Stainless steel fixtures, and white lab coats hung from hooks above a few rust-colored stains. The smell of bleach mixed with the scent of raw flesh and formaldehyde. Overhead the fluorescent lights hummed while the one closest to the door flickered. Cabinets lined the back wall, each one filled with various bottles and tools. I immediately noticed the electric saw and what looked like a hammer.

One bed lay overturned with a table beside it. All the supplies that probably had once sat atop it now were scattered across the stained-brown laminate tile floor. The farthest wall from the entrance was covered with small metal doors that had to be the freezers for the body. A chair braced against one of the door handles gave me a solid idea of where this living dead body waited.

"I'm assuming that's where he is?" I asked, moving towards the cooler.

Jackson nodded as I pulled the chair to the side and yanked the door open. Cold air rushed across me and my skin prickled at the touch.

Pitch black on top of a stainless steel tray, my fingers brushed against an empty body bag that I threw to the side. I slowly reached in and grabbed the edge of the rolling tray, pulling it backwards and out of the cooler. Bound and tied in the center of the metal gurney, a blonde man laid still. Medical tape tied his wrists and ankles together.

His bones showed clearly through his almost transparent yellow-tinted skin. Clumps of his hair had long since fallen off, and one ear was completely gone to decomposition. His clothes consisted of old rags of what looked like a military uniform, but not from any branch I recognized.

I pressed my blade against his cheek. Though the edge cut through skin, no blood dribbled onto it. He groaned softly, his eyes opened to show a pale grey color with a sharp blue center just around the iris. I took a step back, keeping the blade ready.

"You're dead," Jackson said from behind me. "You're a dead man. I checked everything."

The man groaned again, looking from me to Jackson. As soon as his eyes focused on me, he let out a growl, and bit at the medical tape around his wrists. Gnawed to shreds in seconds, he pushed off of the tray, yellow thin fingers grabbing towards us.

Pushing Jackson to the side and out of harm's way, I let my knife slide past his grabbing hands and slammed the blade into his chest before ripping lengthwise across him. His body sizzled as his skin dissolved into dust and everything faded until all that was left was a rag and a small shard of bone.

"What is going on?" Jackson demanded.

I took a deep breath. "It's not something you need to worry about," I said.

"Bull." She crossed her arms. "That man was dead. I checked his stats and cut out his organs myself. There is absolutely no way that he was alive, so how was he up and moving and attacking people! And then you just stab him and POOF! What is going on?"

I opened my mouth to respond when a dull thud sounded from one of the other doors. I froze, knife slowly coming back up. "How many John or Jane Does do you have in here right now?" I asked.

Jackson frowned, then realization slowly hit. She swallowed hard. "I have four unidentified bodies in here. They're all in the coolers waiting for transport. Someone was supposed to be by, but—"

"Alright, Jackson," I said, firming my voice to let the doctor know there was no questioning me, "I'm gonna ask you to take a few steps back and out of the room while I deal with this." I pulled my gun from my hip holster. "And I'll try to not hit any of your equipment."

Jackson nodded slowly, taking several steps backwards and out of the room, closing the main door behind her.

One of the cooler door handles rattled, and I cocked my pistol as I reached forward with my free hand and pulled the door open. "Morning, sunshine," I said as I fired one shot point blank right between the eyes of the dead woman just as her hands reached my throat. Her mouth dropped open and she wheezed once before her skin began to dissolve into nothing but dust that flittered around me.

I heard another two of the doors rip open just before

something grabbed me and jerked hard at my ankle. I groaned and toppled backwards, hitting the ground. One of the dead bodies crawled on top of me. The smell of formaldehyde curled around me as a gaping mouth opened and rotten teeth snapped at me. I felt the bone brittle fingers start curling around my throat, but before they could come close to strangling me, I rammed my elbow upwards, slamming into the creature's gut. Its spit splattered on my cheek as I rolled over and pinned it to the ground with one hand while firing my pistol with the other. It fell apart beneath me and I rolled over.

Two other bodies were just getting to their feet. One rushed toward me, grabbing my wrist and bending it backwards until my gun dropped from my hand.

"Think that's gonna do you a lot of good?" I asked, grabbing at the tools on one of the side tables. My fingers found a hammer. I gripped it and swung.

The hammer cracked the skull of the creature. It howled, releasing my wrist and stumbling backwards, grabbing at its head. It screamed and dust flew from its mouth as it dropped to its knees and exploded into a burst of its former self.

The last one lurched for me, grabbing my shoulders and slamming me into the cooler doors. One of the door handles bore into my back and I groaned, before pushing my knee up and into the groin of the dead man trying to pin me down. He growled but his grip loosened for just a split second. That was all I needed to push him off and send his head slamming into the steel plated cooler doors. Nothing but powdered corpse dropped to the floor.

I coughed and rubbed my throat.

"Jackson? It's alright now."

The doctor came rushing back into the room with a baseball bat in hand, "What? What's happening?"

I raised my hands. "Bat down. There's no need for that," I said.

She slowly lowered the bat. "What are you doing? Who are you?"

"Legitimate questions," I said, "I'm called the Pulptress and I'm here because you called."

"Well I know that much. But why are you here at all? Why did that thing have your information in its hands?"

"That I'm not sure about," I admitted, "but I intend to find out. What can you tell me about these bodies? Where were they found?"

Jackson stammered for a few moments before reaching over and pulling the hammer from my hand and putting it into a nearby sink. "Let me pull out their files," she said as she walked over to a large lateral cabinet and pulled out a collection of files. "I know they were all found within the same 24 hour period. It was a big scandal here. We don't have the kind of crime that say Atlanta or some big city has."

She opened up the first one and nodded. "They were all found not very far from Epsilon First Cemetery." She closed the folder. "I've got their belongings too." She walked over to a separate set of meticulously labeled drawers. She pulled out a few plastic evidence bags. "They all were in really tattered clothes. Police all figured they had to be homeless, probably got into a bad batch of drugs and overdosed."

"And what did your examination turn up?" I asked, picking up one of the bags and looking over the evidence and the ratty clothes.

"I didn't find any trace of drug use, but I took a few blood and tissue samples to send for a tox screen," she answered, then paused and walked over to a small refrigerator where she pulled out several labeled vials. "You have to be kidding me." She sighed as she shook the plastic vial now filled with nothing but a pale, ashy dust.

I looked over the second bag of collected items and spotted a strange sprig of green plant stuck to the bottom of a pant leg. "What's this?" I asked.

Jackson made her way back over to my side. "Hm? Oh yeah, I made a note of that. All of them had some traces of rosemary on them."

"Rosemary?" I asked. "Like the herb you cook with? So what? They all came from some kind of kitchen?"

Jackson crossed her arms. "Rosemary also grows in the wild, and it's one of the most popular plants to grow in a cemetery. Epsilon First has several plots of rosemary."

I nodded. That made it absolutely clear where the Bone Queen was, and that she was back to her old tricks, raising the dead and causing hell, but why here? Why now? I shook my head. "Well thanks. I think I'm going to go check this out. Could you give me directions to this graveyard?"

Jackson chewed at her lip for a few moments before pulling the evidence away from me and putting it back into the file drawer and locking it closed. "I'll go with you."

"Whoa," I said as I held up my hands. "What?"

"I'll go with you," Jackson repeated as she put away the rest of her files.

"I don't think you understand. This isn't a joy ride or a field trip through a cemetery. This is going to be dangerous. You saw those things right? The one just now? The one that attacked you? There will be more of those things."

"I gathered," Jackson said after a moment, "but I am willing to take that risk. Let me get my bag and we'll go." She headed back for the main area of her office and out of the morgue.

I stared for a moment, then followed after her. "You're willing to take that risk? Why?" I asked.

She sighed. "Because I need hard evidence for what just happened or else my job is gone. I've just lost four bodies in my care. Do you think that's going to go over well with the police department?" She shook her head, "I need solid proof so that I keep my job, and don't get taken to the loony bin for claiming that four bodies just dissolved into dust after raising from the dead and attacking." She walked over to her desk, and picked up her purse. "Now, if you're done asking questions, I'd like to get this done before thunderstorms roll in this afternoon."

I sighed, running a hand through my hair. I really didn't need some civilian to have to keep an eye on while trying to go after the Bone Queen, but I needed to get to this cemetery. "Fine, but you stay out of the way and the second I tell you to run, you take off without a word, got it?"

She nodded. "Yes, fine. Don't worry so much. I do know how to fire a gun, and have taken several self-defense classes. I'll be fine," she assured me as she headed out to the rusted out truck in the driveway.

I take a few seconds before I follow after Jackson as she climbs into her truck. I hesitantly settled into the passenger side of the truck. It struggled a few times as Jackson turned the key, then finally the engine turned over and it rumbled to life like a freight train. Shifting gears, Jackson backed out of the driveway and out of the area.

The dirt roads weren't quite as bumpy on the drive in the truck; I didn't feel like my teeth were about to rattle out of my head at least.

"So, what is going on?" Jackson asked.

"I don't think you'd believe it even if I did even if I did tell you." I said after a moment, "Just get me to the cemetery. That's all I need from you."

Jackson frowned, glancing at me before looking back to

the road and taking a left down a gravel road. "So, there's dead things coming to life in my morgue and you're not going to tell me what's going on because you think it's too unbelievable? Unless you tell me you're filming some new episode of reality TV, then I think I'll believe it."

I felt a small smile tug at my lips. "Good point. All right look, there's a woman. I don't know her real name but she's known as The Bone Queen. She raises the dead by eating their bones. I fought her once in Paris, and I'm here to take her out for good. She killed someone very important to me, and I promised I'd hunt her down. That's all you need to know."

"So one person is doing all of this? Some kind of nec-romancer or something?" Jackson asked, turning down another dirt road filled with potholes that bounced the truck.

I braced my hands on the ceiling of the car to keep from slamming into it. "Something like that. You're taking this a lot better than I thought you would honestly."

She took a deep breath. "See, I…" she trailed off then shook her head. "My grandfather use to tell me this story when I was little. He said there was a soldier during the Civil War that had been touched by the devil because he wouldn't die. He told me that he was there, he saw the devil, shot him clean through and the man kept coming." she looked at me as she drove. "He told me that eventually they bound the man in an iron casket and buried him in an unmarked grave here in Epsilon. If there are dead things rising…"

"It's not him. That's some folktale. I know who is behind this and I'm here to stop her," I said. Nothing was going to change my mind.

Those things in the morgue looked exactly like the

chiffoniers I'd faced in Paris, and I had no doubt that it was that woman behind all of this. How one of them had gotten my contact information into its hand was something I still hadn't figured out.

Jackson kept quiet as we pulled into an empty grass lot that served as a parking lot. Low, crumbling brick walls circled the cemetery with at least three old wrought iron gates around the property. An entire section of wall had crumbled to the ground around the back areas. In the distance I could make out what looked like an old church steeple sticking out just above an area of woods around the graves.

"How big is this place?" I asked Jackson as she put it in park.

"Oh a few dozen acres. It's massive." She said, "Heard some developers tried to buy it up but they did a land survey and found miles of tunnels under the graves. Guess it was used as some kind of barricades during the Civil War maybe, no one's found the entrance yet. Most people just think it's an urban legend."

I unbuckled and opened my door before turning to Jackson and telling her, "You should just wait in the truck."

"I'm not waiting in the truck," Jackson scoffed and crossed her arms, "You're hunting dead things and telling me that my story about the dead rising is some fairytale? You don't know any better than I do why those people came back to life!"

I took a deep breath, "I do know better than you. I've dealt with these things before. Now I don't know why they're here, or why one of them had a piece of paper about me, but that's what I'm going to find out. I can't be worried about you wandering around with these things on the attack. Maybe you've missed this somewhere along the line but it's dangerous. There are going to be things, undead things, trying to kill me and anyone with me."

"One of them tried to kill me before I even knew you existed. It was delivered to my morgue with your name and number in its hand. I want to know what's going on just as much as you do. This is my home, and I need to know what's going on or else I can kiss my job goodbye for losing several bodies."

"We can find a way to keep that from happening," I told her. "Your life is more important than your job."

Jackson smiled. "Yeah I know that, but I think with us working together I can keep both of them just fine and figure out what's going on."

I shook my head, but stopped arguing, it was wasting time. Getting out of the truck, it was clear that this grassy parking lot didn't see a lot of traffic. In fact, the only car here besides us was a sleek black car covered in dust and pollen. It'd clearly been here a while without moving.

"Not a real popular place is it?" I asked.

Jackson laughed. "I don't think anyone has been buried here since … phew, maybe the '50s," she said after a moment of thought. "Most of the people buried here are in unmarked graves. Leftovers from the Civil War mainly. My grandfather's out here somewhere."

I frowned. "Unmarked graves?" I asked as I got out of the truck.

Jackson followed behind me. "Yeah, I guess maybe mass graves would be a better term. You see the uneven patches of the ground, the weird hills and valleys. Those are from graves where they just dumped the unclaimed bodies. There are a few actual tombstones, and a few families even have mausoleums." She motioned toward the east side of the cemetery. "But otherwise it's just a collection of unknowns.

Historians come out here from time to time to try to make headway on who's buried here, but most of the time they find nothing but a few abandoned churches about a mile outside the cemetery." She stepped over one of the broken sections of the wall.

I followed behind her and took a quick look around the cemetery. The ground sloped and fell in chaotic, unnatural patterns, and in the distance I could see a few dark shapes that must have been the tombs and graves Jackson had mentioned. Of all the mass graves in the world, why was the Bone Queen here in Epsilon, Georgia?

Jackson walked away from the wall and into the cemetery. She took a deep breath. "Rosemary is this way," she called over her shoulder.

I let my hand rest on the butt of my gun and headed after her. "You think the rosemary will lead us to where those things came from?"

She nodded. "It's a good place to start unless you'd rather just wander the cemetery looking for dead things."

I frowned but didn't respond as we tracked through the graveyard. I caught the scent of the rich, warm tang of rosemary crisp against the humid air and pushed past Jackson, taking over the lead.

Over a hill we came to a patch of wild, overgrown rosemary, thick spiked plants grabbing at the edges of my pants and sticking to them. Jackson knelt beside me and pulled a small plastic Ziploc bag from her purse and carefully collected a few pieces.

"What are you doing?" I asked.

"If I can get a match of this to the plants that were on those bodies that will confirm they came from here inside the cemetery. It's a start at least," she said, putting the evidence back into her bag.

Overhead dark clouds rumbled. Jackson pulled her white leather jacket tighter around herself. "We need to find something and get out of here before the storm breaks."

"I'm not going anywhere," I said, reaching into the bushes and trying to feel through the tangles of branches and clinging pine-like needles to see if there was any sort of hole or trap door hidden there. "This isn't a mystery that needs to be solved. This is a simple case of finding the person doing this and stopping her."

Jackson huffed. "Alright, fine. You want to putz around a cemetery in a thunderstorm, that's—"

I froze as something seized my arm and jerked me forward. I nearly toppled into the rosemary bushes, but Jackson grabbed the back of my shirt, then my arm and pulled me back. Another hard yank and me and the thing holding onto me flew backwards and crashed into the ground into a pile.

I scrambled for my gun as Jackson and the thing still holding onto my wrist, struggled to get upright.

Abandoning trying to get to free my gun from my hoodie, I finally settled for my knife and slashed at the hand holding onto me. It jerked backwards and I followed, pressing my blade into the pale neck of a gaunt, blonde man.

"Wait a second!" Jackson grabbed my arm, "Wait, don't just—"

"Who are you?" I demanded.

The man was dirty with a sickly yellow coloring to his skin. He didn't move like one of those dead things, but he didn't seem totally alive. His eyes were dark and the cut on his hand from my knife didn't bleed. I tightened my hand on the blade and readied it to plunge into his chest, "Speak now if you can."

He spoke with a faint smirk. "I thought I saw an angel."

I sputtered and the knife pressed against his chest, ready

to pierce him as I said, "What did you just say to me?"

"If you are not interested, that's all you had to say." He offered a smile "I can handle 'no'."

"Stop!" Jackson hissed. "Get your knife away from him!" She grabbed at my arm but I easily avoided her grasp.

I pulled the blade to his throat. "Stop with the cutesy act. You can talk, so talk. What are you doing here? Where did you come from?"

"Oh, shall I tell you about my childhood? What an awful time that was," he said with a grin. A very faint French accent hid under his words.

"Jackson, check him for a pulse." I said, pulling my knife off of his throat, and instead taking out my gun to aim at him. "One wrong move, and you're gone." I told him.

He just smiled and stayed still as Jackson pressed her fingers to his throat, then his wrist, and finally to his chest. She leaned back, looking to me and then to him. "I can't find one. I swear he doesn't have one."

"And you would be swearing correctly. I am dead. Quite dead in fact," he said before sitting up with a soft groan.

"Then how are you talking?" Jackson asked.

"Ah, well, there's the trick. I may be technically dead, but my body keeps on moving. What is that saying? The spirit is willing but the body won't? Something like that?" His smile split crooked across his face.

"Who are you?" I pulled back the hammer on the gun. "Tell me."

"Name's Aramis," he said, looking up at me. "And you must be The Pulptress."

"How do you know me?" I demanded.

"It isn't hard. You've earned a reputation, particularly your bone hunting ways," he said with a wink.

"You know about her? About what happened in France?"

I dropped the gun down just an inch.

"*Est-ce que je connais la France?*" He laughed, "Oh, I know more about what happened in France and about her than you ever will. I know that she killed someone very dear to you in Paris. Do I need to say more than that?" He tilted his head faintly.

"What is going on?" Jackson demanded.

I took a deep breath and reluctantly put the gun away. "The woman I told you about who killed my mentor."

"I know that woman," Aramis added, "Well, knew," he corrected. "We haven't spoken in oh a good thousand years or so at least. Since the last time we tried to kill each other probably." He shrugged.

"You've tried to kill her?" I asked, "How? How do you kill something that's already dead?"

"That's the problem," he said. "I can't."

"But?" Jackson prodded.

He smiled. "First I think getting out before it rains might be in order. Rotted skin and water don't mix well." He pointed up toward the sky then slowly got to his feet. He stumbled and Jackson steadied him.

He closed his eyes with a faint groan as thunder rumbled again.

"I think we have guests," he said.

"What?" My gun was out and at the ready again, and it only took me a second to see the horde of stumbling chiffoniers. "We need to go now!" I said, grabbing Jackson's arm and pulling her back toward the parking lot.

2

JACKSON STUMBLED AFTER ME, and the strange man followed right behind her. I didn't bother trying to count the number of creatures coming toward us. I could hear their steps against the soggy ground and see glimpses of shadows moving with every bolt of lightning striking near us. As the rain rushed over us in a near torrential downpour, I struggled to keep Jackson with me, and, paying more attention to who was behind me than what was in front of me, I plowed straight into a headstone and toppled to the ground with the air knocked out of me.

Jackson tripped over me and fell to the ground, skidding across the damp clay.

I grunted and tried to get back to my feet, but struggled with the slick mud clinging to my shoes. The man, Aramis, appeared in another flash of lightning, grabbing my hand and helping to pull me to my feet. I used his grip as a counter weight and jerked myself upright and then backwards, shoving myself into the chest of one creature that had gotten a bit too close. However, another grabbed a fistful of my hair and jerked me backwards. I stumbled back toward the approaching horde.

"Go!" I yelled at Jackson and the man.

Jackson picked up her baseball bat and charged forward swinging. The man stayed where he was.

Jackson's bat cracked through several fragile skulls, and dusty remains of the chiffoniers splattered in thick clumps against my cheek. Letting loose of her weapon with one hand, Jackson took my arm. "Come on!" She pulled me.

I let her drag me ahead as I tightened my grip on my pistol and fired at anything that got too close. Aramis rejoined us as we crawled over the brick wall and rushed toward the truck as another group chased after us.

"Get in the back!" Jackson yelled as she scrambled to unlock the truck's door and get into the driver's side. I jumped into the bed of the truck with Aramis right behind me. I fired a few shots at some of the creatures as they screamed and reached for us. "Jackson!!" I roared.

"I'm trying!" She yelled back, the engine sputtered several times before finally turning over. Tires squealed and tore through the mud, knocking a few more chiffoniers back from the truck as it tore toward the road.

I grabbed onto the side railing and Aramis did the same as the truck bounced wildly, and the rain just made the metal bed slicker. My grip kept slipping and I slid closer toward the end of the truck bed and a drop straight onto the gravel road.

Aramis reached out and offered his hand, and after a few seconds of hesitation I grabbed it.

He wrapped his fingers around my wrist and swung me back toward the top of the truck. I grabbed onto the open window in the back of the cab and held on tightly as we swerved through the muddy roads, and finally back onto solid asphalt. I let out a deep breath and squinted back through the pouring rain, sure that we were safe for the moment.

We drove the rest of the way in silence and when the truck finally pulled into the driveway, I eagerly jumped back onto solid ground. Jackson hurried to the front door and opened it up. "Here get inside. I think I have some spare scrubs you two can change into and I'll throw your clothes in the wash."

I nodded and stood in the hallway, sopping wet and dripping all over the hardwood floors. Jackson hurried inside and then returned with royal blue scrubs that she handed to me and then to Aramis.

He took his and went to find a side room to change in. "Here, there's a restroom right here." Jackson pointed a door out to me. "Just leave your clothes on the floor and I'll collect them in a minute."

I nodded and slipped into the bathroom. Shutting and locking the door behind me, I slowly began to peel my sopping wet clothes off and flung them to the ground. The warm, dry scrubs felt like heaven against my skin. I sighed, and padded barefoot back out into the hallway to see Aramis joining Jackson as well. She walked past me and grabbed my wet laundry before tucking Aramis' clothes under her arm and going down the hallway.

"You have a washer here?" I asked.

"We do have running water in Georgia, you know," Jackson teased. "Yeah, sometimes the autopsies can get a little messy." She smiled. "So it's a good idea to keep something here to help with that."

"Thank you," Aramis said with a nod.

He looked toward me, and stepped closer to my side as Jackson turned the corner and began loading the washing machine.

"I think I've found a way to kill the Bone Queen." He

said. "But it can only be done by the hand of the living."

"Well, that seems obvious." Jackson huffed, looking back around the corner. "The dead don't…" she looked at Aramis, "…aren't suppose to be able to do much of anything, let alone kill someone!"

I didn't comment as Jackson disappeared down the hallway to another room to change her clothes. Aramis offered me a smile.

I didn't return it and turned to face him. "Who are you?"

He smiled, "Aramis. Your friendly, neighborhood helping hand."

"What are you doing here?" I asked.

"Same as you." He said.

I narrowed my eyes, "Were you there in Paris?"

His smile faded a bit, "No. I wasn't there, but I've been tracking her for a long time. It wasn't hard to notice when someone else began following her signs."

"You've been watching me?" My hand slid towards the hilt of my knife.

"Not in the peeping-Tom sort of way. I mean you're a lovely woman but I'm dead, and you're not… it just wouldn't work." He teased.

My face stayed stony, and he cleared his throat then sighed. "You really need to work on your sense of humor. Yes, I was watching you, mainly where you were going. Atlanta, right? That's where your information had her heading from Europe. You were on the right track. You just missed where she went from the airport. Not a big deal." He shrugged.

"And I take it you didn't miss where she was heading?" I asked. "How? How did you know where she was going?"

He hesitated before saying, "Let's just say we have an intimate connection that gives me better information on what she's doing than any detective work ever could."

"So you came here and then what? Planted my information?"

"I knew that'd get your attention." He said, "I figured if it came from someone who had no clue what was going on you'd be more likely to come."

"You could have killed someone by letting those chiffoniers be collected!"

"It was fine!" He waved his hand dismissively. "We're in rural Georgia, babies know how to shoot guns here. But I will say that whole protect the innocent thing you've got? Really great trait by the way."

"What do you want?" I finally asked.

"I want the same as you," he said simply.

"And what's that?" I demanded.

"To stop the Bone Queen. That should be obvious."

"You just said that wasn't possible, that you can't kill her," I protested.

"No, I said I can't kill something that's already dead," he said with a smile. "Now you on the other hand, well there's hope for you being able to."

Jackson walked up with a plateful of sandwiches. "Hungry?" she asked.

I frowned but took a sandwich and slowly sat down at the table. Aramis sat across from me and Jackson joined us.

"What are you two talking about?" she asked.

I looked to Aramis.

He offered a smile. "So this is where the creatures were taken. Where were they held? May I see?"

Jackson looked at me then nodded, and stood up. Aramis and I followed her back down to the autopsy chambers. He looked around with a slow nod.

"So, are you actually dead?" Jackson asked, watching

Aramis.

"Hm?" He glanced at her. "In your sense of the word, I am very dead. No pulse means no life, correct?"

Jackson said, "Then how are you able to move? What kind of circulatory system provides blood for your muscles to be able—"

Aramis laughed. "Ah, I see. You are one of the science minded people. Very admirable, but unfortunately entirely lacking in the means to describe how it is I still move." He explained, "I move because it is willed to happen. Willed by something very close to death. My body is far past the point of death, but it stays, partially because of this Bone Queen you hunt."

"Who is she?" Jackson asked.

"She is exactly who she sounds like. A creature of bone and hate," Aramis said after a moment. "And I have the means to destroy her."

I protested, "But I thought you said—"

"I said I had failed at killing her. That does not mean it isn't possible," he interrupted. "I am not so proud that I don't realize sometimes I am out of my depth."

"So what do you need?" I asked.

"I need a living soul."

"Like a sacrifice?" Jackson asked as she circled around him.

"No, not like a sacrifice at all." He said with a sigh.

"Do you mind?" Jackson asked as she pulled a stethoscope from her desk.

He shook his head. "By all means my dear."

Jackson put the stethoscope against his back, frowning.

"What did you mean you need a living soul?" I asked. "Like a sacrifice?"

He laughed, "No, nothing quite as dark as that. Someone

living has to be the one to kill her. It doesn't work if another dead does it, believe me I have tried."

"What do we have to do?"

"There are three gems. I've got one, and she's got one in the sword she keeps with her."

"And the third?" I pressed.

"I think it is somewhere in the cemetery here. It became some kind of family heirloom and when that family went from France to England to America, it came with them. But she and I lost track of it during the Civil War."

"You both know where it is?" I asked.

"Why else would we be in the middle of nowhere Georgia?" He smiled.

"And what? You just start digging up the graves?" Jackson asked, shaking her head. "That's not going to happen."

"I didn't say anything about digging," Aramis said. "My gem will let me know when we get close to it and the last time I went down to the cemetery I could tell it's somewhere in there, but I knew I needed help." He turned to face me. "So, I got help."

I nodded, crossing my arms and drumming my fingers against my forearms.

"Are you considering helping him?" Jackson asked.

"Yes. He's my ticket to finding the monster that killed Amaury." I curled my fingers into a fist. "You got a deal." I nodded to Aramis.

He flashed a smile. "Well then, I guess now we just need a plan."

"What do you know about the gem?" I asked.

"I know it's relatively small, small enough to fit in the palm of your hand. It'll either be grey or black, and when it gets close to my gem, I'll know."

"Where's the one you have then?" I asked, watching

Jackson move around the room out of the corner of my eye.

"Well, I can't exactly show it to you."

"And why not?" I asked, crossing my arms.

"Well, it's—OW!" He jumped as Jackson poked a needle into his arm, sucking a small amount of blood into the plunger and then pulling away. "What are you doing? Give some warning before hand at least." He rubbed his arm.

Jackson muttered to herself as she went over to some of her equipment. I watched her for a moment before turning back to Aramis. "So this gem. What else can you tell me?"

"It's old," he said, still rubbing his arm, "and she'll be looking for it too. I know she's here somewhere, I can feel it. When I was in the cemetery I could feel her watching me, but she's starting to lose power. It's too hard for her to hide what she is, her skin fails."

"She never hid it in Paris," I muttered.

"Well, I imagine that flying across the ocean as a half skeleton must be a challenge," he said with a smirk. "You eventually learn and figure out a way to make it work I guess. No one checks for a pulse to get on a plane and enough money can buy the necessary fake documents to get anyone through."

"So she knows this gem is here too? She'll be searching for it as well," I said.

"You've got it." Aramis smiled. "But since she's here, if we find it before her, we can use it to kill her for good."

"And if she finds it before us?"

"Well then she'll probably go after me and my gem and if she gets that she'll use the three of them together to summon a plague that will wipe out most of the world and turn all the dead into her army."

"What?" Jackson spoke up from her corner.

Aramis glanced toward her. "Yeah I know, it is—"

"This is incredible." Jackson said.

"Those are not the words I would have used," Aramis said with a frown.

"What are you talking about?" I asked.

"This blood, it's … This is incredible!" Jackson murmured, half to herself and half to the rest of the room. "It's dead, but still moving. The cells don't regenerate but they still create. It's amazing."

"Well thank you. I do what I can," Aramis grinned.

"Do you realize what kind of advancement this kind of work could cause?" she asked. "Being able to keep dead cells active?"

"I'm assuming a lot, but that isn't going to happen," Aramis said. "It's a side effect of a cursed gem."

"Which I'm still waiting to see," I butted in. "Where is yours?"

He sighed. "It's embedded in my chest. I wanted to make sure it stayed safe. Forever. So I made sure I could never lose it. Looking back on it, it was a poor decision, but at the time it made sense."

"How long have you been alive?" Jackson asked.

"Um …" Aramis looked at the ceiling, counting on his fingers. "I don't know exactly. Since the first black plague in France? All the years start to blur together anymore."

"All the things you must have seen." Jackson leaned against the table. "I can't imagine. You're … truly dead. This isn't some kind of trick?"

"Truly dead." He smiled. "I promise."

Jackson frowned, walking back over to him, and looked him over carefully. "But there are no signs of decomposition."

"None," he agreed.

I rubbed my temples. "Yes, this is all very fascinating, but what I want to know is more about this gem. We need to know where it is. We can't just blindly wander the graveyard until you get a feeling in your chest."

"That isn't what I suggested doing," Aramis protested.

"It sure sounded like it to me." I crossed my arms. "What do you suggest then?"

"Going to the graveyard and doing a walk around getting a feeling of the general area where the gem should be, and then carefully digging." He said with a smile.

"You can't dig up those graves!" Jackson spoke from her workbench. "That's illegal."

"Well, in case you missed it, we're fighting someone that kills people so I think bending the law a little is alright," Aramis pointed out. "In the name of saving the world a few laws must be broken. Hopefully the judge will be lenient on a corpse like me."

I rubbed my temples and let out a long sigh. "So yeah, we do need to wander around aimlessly until you just get a good feeling about this gem? God, that has got to be the worst plan I've ever heard."

"Well then, what's yours?" Aramis asked.

I frowned. "I don't know! I don't know how this all—" I paused when I heard something thump from the entryway. "Jackson? You expecting company?"

3

Jackson looked up from her work. "It might be one of the officers, they come check on me from time to time. I'll go see." She wiped her hands on her lab coat and headed up the stairs.

I lingered at the bottom of the hallway and listened. The door eased open and I could make out the muffled sound of Jackson's voice, and then another loud thud. Jackson's voice got louder and then I heard a distinct crash of something shattering. Drawing my pistol, I rushed her way.

Jackson stood above a pile of dust and bones at her feet, mingled with the shattered remains of a lamp. "He … It attacked me," she said slowly, taking several slow deep breaths. "They must've followed us from the graveyard."

"Get back into the basement," I told her, pushing her behind me.

She stumbled toward the stairs as I hurried to check the rest of the floor. The rooms were empty, though I found one broken window with some ripped fabric on it that marked the monster's entry point. The rain from outside poured in as the lightning crashed and thunder roared. Looking into the backyard, I found it crawling with stumbling creatures.

I pulled my pistol from my pocket, and loaded it with the extra bullets I kept along my belt before I took a position under the broken window. Aiming through the broken panes of glass, I fired, taking out the closest creature. It dropped to the ground in a heap of filth.

The noise sent the other monsters clawing for me. One moved faster than others grabbing my hand, digging its nail into the soft flesh of my wrist. I grunted with pain as my hand lost grip on my pistol and dropped it. I managed to get my other arm up and slammed my elbow into the creature's nose. It released me and stumbled backwards.

I took the chance to step away from the window as one of the monsters began clawing through. Pulling my knife from its sheath, I slashed across its throat. It groaned, then dissolved. The next two went down just as fast, but then the door behind me burst open and more of them rushed. I dropped to the floor, just barely missing the grabbing hands.

Cutting Achilles' tendons as I went, I crawled from the room. The monsters toppled above me, still clawing and grabbing. One got firm hold of my boot. I pulled my leg back and slammed it crashing into the thing's shoulder again and again, until the thin arm separated free from the rest of its body.

Grabbing my pistol as I escaped the room and rolled back to my feet, kicking the skeleton hand still clinging to me free from my pants. Several more rushed toward me and I stumbled backwards. I snagged my finger around the trigger and fired into the mouth of the closest monster lunging toward me, its toothless mouth agape.

The bullet took out its intended target and the three behind it before embedding in the wall of the bedroom. I took the moment of confusion to rush out of the hallway where more monsters were pushing out of the bedrooms.

Windows shattered all around me as they crawled in from all sides, swarming. Was she sending them after me or after Aramis I wondered, glancing toward the basement door, still closed and unscathed. I turned my attention back to the task at hand and raised my pistol.

I fired three quick shots, knocking the closest group down before running into the hallway and slamming the door behind me. The closed door slowed down the hordes enough for me to reload the gun. As the door was ripped open, I fired into the masses. The last three dissolved into nothing but dust.

After the last of the dust and bones hit the floor, the house fell quiet. I headed to the back door and let out a breath when I saw the backyard sitting empty once again. I slid my gun back into my pocket and drew out my knife from the holster around my waist as I stepped out the door and into the rain. "A cake walk," I muttered to myself.

I never saw what hit me. Pain just exploded across the back of my head and I slammed into the ground with a groan. My knives toppled into the soaked clay as I struggled to get my bearings and try to get back to my feet. Cold hands closed around my neck, squeezing tighter and tighter as I wheezed and struggled.

The world started to grow dark as I clawed at the ground, finding enough dirt in the area to fling a handful backwards. It loosened the grip around my neck enough for me to take a gasp of cool air and get my senses back somewhat.

I slammed my head backwards, cracking the already throbbing back of my head against the nose of someone behind me. The figure groaned and let go. I grabbed one of my knives and rolled backwards to jump to my feet.

The dead man staring at me wore what looked like an old Civil War Confederate gray uniform, and he groaned, clawing at his busted nose, cracked and revealing slivers of his skull through his thin skin. Not waiting for him to recover, I slammed my blade into his eye until he dissolved into dust that melted under the rain.

Beside me I heard something crack against bone and turned in time to see Jackson with a baseball bat in her hand, swinging wildly as the dead swarmed around her.

Aramis stood beside her with an old, partially rusted sword in hand, cutting down any that came too close. In a matter of moments the two had knocked down the rest of the dead.

I cleared my throat. "Nice help," I croaked out.

"Are you alright?" Jackson walked to my side, putting her hand to my shoulder. I tilted my chin up to let her look over my throat.

"Just sore," I said.

She nodded, gingerly touching at my throat. "It will be bruised, and your voice is going to be a bit rough."

"I'll live somehow," I said with a roll of my eyes. "Let's get out of this rain."

Jackson shook her head and began collecting the bones dropped around the yard.

"You're pretty good with those little daggers of yours," Aramis commented, walking over to me, helping me up and heading inside.

I followed after him. "Practice," I explained with a shrug, rubbing the back of my head, grateful no blood coated the back of my hand. The last thing I needed was some head wound slowing me down. "What did he even hit me with?" I muttered.

"The butt of a musket," Aramis answered, pointing to the pile of dust where a rusted old gun laid on the grass.

"Of course." I sighed. "I guess this means she really is

here," I said, glancing at Aramis.

He looked up at the setting sun. "If you had any doubts before I guess this is proof enough?"

I nodded. "Not unless anyone else can summon these things."

"God I hope not." Aramis said.

"Almost all of these bones have rosemary with them," Jackson said, walking back up with a pile of bones and the small green herb in her hands.

"And?"

"Well I think that almost confirms that they came from the cemetery. That's really the only place you can get rosemary in this amount. This is fresh from a bush. It must have stuck to them when they left the cemetery." Jackson mused, "God, these bones are ancient."

"Yeah, I bet they are," I muttered, picking up a bone she'd missed, and running it over in my fingers. The touch of time was all over these bones, picked clean and smooth over the years in the ground.

"Going to the cemetery in the dead of the night in a thunderstorm when we're thinking we're going to run into more of those things is not a good idea." She frowned at me.

"Time's not exactly on our side." I said as I checked my pistol.

"If she finds that gem before us that won't lead to anything good. The more gems she has, the stronger the creatures she revives will be," Aramis said. "She can summon the dead innately, but with two gems … anything that she raises from the dead will be touched by the power of her blasted goddess."

I turned to Aramis. "You know a lot more about this than you let on at the beginning of all of this."

Aramis cleared his throat as thunder roared overhead.

Jackson looked between Aramis and me before jumping when a raindrop hit her. "Let's get back inside. I need your help getting this place put back together. I can't really tell the police that a bunch of zombies attacked me and that's why it's a mess."

I waited until Jackson had stepped inside and Aramis had followed her to go after them. I didn't want Aramis at my back.

I began working on getting the rooms put back together. Jackson swept up the broken pieces of furniture, plates, and lamps while Aramis got the desk flipped back upright and tried to put some of the things back into place.

"What are you going to tell them about all the windows being broken?" I asked as Jackson carefully collected the broken glass and tossed it into the trash.

Jackson shrugged her shoulders. "Storms break all kinds of things."

I grinned. "Smart girl."

"Not a girl. A doctor," Jackson pointed out as she straightened the display case with her diploma in it.

"My bad." I held up my hands.

Jackson turned back toward me. "How do you do it?"

"Do what?" I asked as I shoved a bookcase back into place.

"Everything that you do."

I laughed. "Well that's the vaguest question I've ever heard."

Jackson sighed. "I mean how do you keep at hunting all these things?"

Frowning, I crossed my arms over my chest. "She took someone from me, and I'm going to make sure she never takes anyone from anyone else every again."

"I just still don't really understand all of this." Jackson shook her head. "But I want to help."

"You what?" I asked, staring at her.

"I want to help you find her," she said again. "Partially out of professional curiosity you understand. I've done the autopsies of thousands of bodies, and never had a one come back to life on me, but this woman is raising things from the dead. It's incredible."

"Yeah, forgive me if I don't see it as such a marvel," I muttered.

"I don't mean that it's a great thing, but I don't understand how she does this, and I never let anything stump me. Besides, I know the cemetery and I think you could use a local guide."

"Oh yeah? They make coroners take classes there?" I asked.

She rolled her eyes. "First, I'm a medical examiner, no one votes for me, and secondly, no. I was a history major for my undergraduate degree. My main focus was on cemeteries so I went into focus on the cemetery right here. I can tell you where just about every major grave site is and I'll know if something doesn't look right."

I frowned. Having someone who knew the area would be helpful, a lot more helpful than dragging Aramis around alone and hoping that eventually he got a 'feeling' that the gem was close. Sighing, I nodded. "Yeah, help would be nice."

Jackson smiled and offered her hand. "Besides, we women have to help one another because frankly, I don't think Aramis could find his way out of a wet paper bag on his own."

I laughed. "He does seem a little dense."

"I heard that!" Aramis called from the hallway, "You two stop talking about me!"

Jackson smiled. "Look, I may not be a great shot but I know how to use a gun, and I know enough about how a body works to keep myself safe. Besides," she swung the bat, "I played second base on the softball team until I was 22. I've got a mean swing."

I sighed and shook my head. I could see enough of myself in Jackson that I knew better than to just say no. "If I don't agree to let you go with me, you're just going to do it on your own, aren't you?"

Jackson shrugged, putting her hands on her hips. "I didn't get into medical school by doing just what I had permission to do."

I smiled. "Alright fine. I've got a pistol I'll let you use, but you don't use it except as a last resort, all right? If we run into trouble then you run, got it?"

Jackson laughed. "Heroics are not my thing, don't worry."

"Are you two done having a moment yet?" Aramis asked, leaning in the doorway.

"Don't get jealous," Jackson walked by Aramis, patting his cheek.

He stammered, and I laughed before going after her.

4

"**I**'VE GOT A FEW maps of the cemetery we can look over tonight while this storm is out there, and tomorrow morning we can start going to the area and hitting up the best spots, but at least looking at the map we won't be going in totally blind." Jackson said.

"And waiting for a 'feeling' about where to go." I glanced at Aramis.

He sighed. "Look, I know it sounds ridiculous but that's about all we have to go on." He scratched the back of his head. "Well, it glows when it gets close to the other gems, but I don't think you'll really be able to see that."

"What? It glows?" Jackson perked up. "How?"

"What do you mean how? It just lights up!" Aramis frowned, taking a step back from the doctor as she approached him.

"Does it heat up?" she asked.

"I guess so." He took another step back. "What are you doing?"

"Where exactly is the gem?" I spoke up.

"It's where my heart used to be," he admitted. "I had to make sure it was somewhere safe."

"The heart," Jackson murmured, tapping her chin before going to a different bedroom.

I could hear her shuffling through something. Occasional bits of plastic or metal hit the floor and rolled across the hallway before she rejoined us with a pair of goggles in her hands.

"One of the deputies left these." She smiled. "Thermal vision goggles."

"Thermal what?" Aramis frowned.

"They let whoever is wearing them see how hot or cold something is," I tried to explain.

She held the goggles up to her eyes and looked over Aramis, stepping slowly closer, and putting a hand to his chest just over his heart. "This is the only part of you that's even close to a regular base human temperature. That's your gem?"

"Yes." He said.

"So it's already warm?" I asked. "That means the other gems are close?"

"I suppose?" Jackson looked to Aramis.

He nodded. "Yeah, that's how I know it's here. I can feel it."

"So the closer we get, the hotter that spot is going to get?" I asked.

Aramis leaned against the wall. "Yes," he finally answered.

"So, will destroying these gems destroy her completely?" I asked.

He bit at the side of his mouth. "I don't know for sure. I know it will limit her power, but most importantly it will keep her from being able to summon a plague."

"A plague?" Jackson took the goggles back off.

Aramis nodded. "Your history books called it The Black Death."

"Wait, so she summoned the Black Plague?" I asked. "How is that—"

"No. No." He shook his head and sighed. "What happened doesn't matter now, but she didn't do that. She … stopped it."

"What are you talking about?" I frowned.

"She wasn't always like this. She just wanted to stop what was happening, and got too caught up in it, in the power." Aramis' voice softened. "I don't think she ever wanted things to go like this. And, if there's any part of that girl left then I owe it to her to stop her from bringing this plague back to earth."

"What?" Jackson frowned. "Okay, the plague was not caused by magic, it was—"

"All those the plague killed came back to life and began to raze the world," Aramis cut her off. "She stood to stop that, to keep the dead truly dead. She wanted that more than anything." He clenched his fists, and then let out a deep breath.

"I don't care about how this all happened," I said. "I just need to know how to stop her from raising anything else from the ground. Is there some special way the gems have to be destroyed?"

"They can only be destroyed by the touch of a living creature," Aramis said. "They can be damaged and disrupted by a touch like mine, but the only way to rid the world of them is for a living soul to destroy them. I've tried, and seen it tried by others, and it never stops the gems, just delays the inevitable."

Jackson sighed. "Well, I'm going to get some supplies together for this cemetery exploration. You both are welcome to stay here for the night. There are couches upstairs that I think escaped destruction."

I didn't think I'd be able to sleep, but accepted the offer any way. "Trying to sleep wouldn't be a bad idea I suppose."

Jackson led me upstairs to one of the only rooms to escape assault by the attacking chiffoniers. Two small twin beds with paisley sheets sat in the middle of the room.

"Why do you have a bedroom here anyways?" I asked.

Jackson shrugged. "Sometimes I stay the night, work gets busy. Sometimes officers need a place to sleep for an hour or two. I had the extra space in this building, might as well put it to better use than yet another storage closet."

I nodded. "Thanks for your help, and for contacting me."

She smiled. "Thanks for actually coming here and not cussing me out and calling me crazy over the phone. That's what I was expecting to happen to be honest. How many people would believe that a dead man came to life with your information in his hands?"

I laughed. "Well, maybe you got lucky this time." I dug through my bag and found the smallest pistol I had. I put it in her hands, "This is for you. This is the safety, don't turn that off unless you're about to shoot something, and don't point at anything you don't want destroyed. This won't do a lot of damage, but it packs enough of a kick to get those things away from you long enough to let you run." I put some rounds in her hand.

She looked at the gun, pointing it toward the wall and testing the weight and movement. "I haven't been shooting since I was little. My dad use to take me."

"Then you've got some experience," I said, "Good, that'll help. And I hope that you don't have to use it."

"If those things are attacking the house then I can't imagine what the cemetery is going to look like."

I offered, "They tend to attack when it's dark. We're going to be there bright and early. She might be cruel and crazy but she isn't stupid. She's not going to send her entire horde out in the middle of the day to chase us from the cemetery." I hoped I was right. I wasn't sure what the Bone Queen was capable of anymore.

Jackson nodded. "Keep the door locked just in case something does come in the night."

"Don't worry I will. Where are you going?" I asked.

"I'm going to set up a room for Aramis then I'll be down in the lab for a while getting some things together, and then I'll probably join you up here. I've got a key for the room so don't worry."

"I apologize in advance for probably pointing a gun at you whenever you come in here. Habit," I explained.

She nodded. "Get some sleep Miss Pulptress."

"There's no 'miss'." I reminded her.

"Honey, in the south, everyone's a miss or a missus," she said with a smile and left the room.

I sighed and put my pistol on the bedside table in easy arm's reach. I closed my eyes and tried counting backwards from 100 to get to sleep, but every number just flashed like bone shapes in front of my eyes. I groaned and pulled the blankets up over my head, but sleep resisted me.

I was still tossing and turning when I heard the key turn in the lock, and the door slowly squeak open. I peered out from under the covers and tracked Jackson as she tiptoed into the room and into the other bed. She sighed heavily, taking her hair band out of her hair with a yawn and flopping into the bed. Within a few seconds, I could hear her softly snoring.

I laid in silence, staring at the ceiling, and taking slow deep breaths. Eventually my eyes closed and I drifted off.

I woke to a raven screeching outside of the window.

"Mmm … What is that?" Jackson grumbled, sitting up.

"Raven." I sighed and slowly got out of bed. "We should get going. Looks like the storm has let up."

Jackson nodded and yawned, putting her feet on the floor and stretching. "And we need to go before someone from the police department comes looking for those bodies."

I rubbed my temples. "Go get Aramis, I'll get my things and then we'll get out of here."

Jackson nodded and disappeared off down the hallway. I took a deep breath before quickly changing into jeans and a plain white t-shirt. I pulled my hair up into a tight ponytail to hold it out of my face. Loading up my bag, I double-checked that I had everything I could think of for any kind of adventure with the undead. Guns, bullets, knives, baton, and a few flashlights. The only thing I hadn't brought was a shovel because that was a pain to carry around on. "Jackson?" I called down the hallway, "Do you have a shovel?"

"A shovel?" Aramis answered. "Are you going to bury me?'

"If only," I replied. "I figure a shovel might be helpful if we find anything needing digging up, like a gem."

"I've got one in the closet by the back door," Jackson called, coming back up from the basement with Aramis behind her.

I went down the hallway and grabbed the shovel, an old, rusted one, but it would work well enough. Tossing it to Aramis, I tightened the bag straps over my shoulders and around my waist to hold it securely in place. Aramis gets the shovel secured to his back, strapping it into place.

"You driving?" I asked Jackson.

Jackson nodded. "We can take the truck." She and I

both looked at Aramis. "You ride in the bed," Jackson said.

"The what?" Aramis asked.

"The back of the truck," I explained.

He frowned, but didn't argue as Jackson grabbed her bag and headed out of the house. Jackson threw her own bag of supplies over her shoulders, a baseball bat stuck out of the top flap of her supplies. She locked the door behind us, and opened up the truck. I threw my bag into the truck bed, and Aramis climbed in to sit beside my stuff.

I nodded, "Keep my stuff secured."

Aramis grinned, and nodded. "Sure thing."

I got into the passenger side and shut the door behind me. Jackson started the truck and headed down the road.

5

LANCING IN THE REARVIEW mirror, I watched Aramis cling to the side railings and flop around in the back of the truck. When we finally got off of the rough dirt road and onto solid, relatively smooth asphalt, Aramis and I both let out a long sigh of relief.

Jackson pulled into the gravel lot. and hopped out. "Alright, best bet is for us to start at the main entrance and work through the three areas of the cemetery."

"How many are buried here?" I asked.

"Depends on what historian you ask," Jackson answered after a moment. "Most of these bodies came from the Civil War, most of them fleeing Sherman when he burned Georgia top to bottom. There weren't a whole lot of options for burials so mass graves were started."

"Why all the rosemary here?" I asked.

"Rosemary's used to say that someone won't be forgotten. It's a nice way to keep a memory alive. You know, they do say that scent is the sense most closely connected to memory," Jackson explained.

"Nothing around here looks disturbed. Not from any-thing but a storm at least," I finally said after we had circled the entryway.

Jackson knelt by the rosemary busy, cutting a small piece and carefully putting it into a plastic evidence bag. "We can try the old slave burial grounds next. That's just right past that last hill there in the back." She put the rosemary sample into her bag and led the way across the field.

"How frequently do people visit?" I asked. "Any chance anyone's seen anything?"

"Visit here?" Jackson sighed, "God, I don't know. Not very much. It's not exactly a thriving tourist attraction and this isn't a real big metropolis, you know."

I nodded, letting out a long breath as we passed a small wall and another statue, this one a granite carving of a flame reaching upwards.

Jackson walked past the statue. "Grandpa's out here somewhere. Or at least that's what we think. There aren't really any records of where he died."

"So the burials here are unknown? How many?" Aramis asked.

"Um … Well yeah, most of the ones here are unknown. There's a sort of listing of the names of some of those believed to be here, but it's nothing confirmed. A lot of slaves, freed slaves, and anyone whose skin was a hair too dark got dropped out here. I guess it's lucky some of them even got a burial." Jackson shrugged.

"Nothing looks disturbed out here either," I said. "The grounds have no recent holes."

Jackson shook her head. "No it doesn't. I guess someone pulling up bodies would be kind of obvious, let alone the effort and mess you'd make just digging through the clay."

"What was the third section you mentioned?" Aramis

asked.

Jackson ran her hand along the stone statue, tracing the smooth lines with her fingers, playing over the rough granite. "It's the old money section. All the mausoleums and big graves are there."

She led the way to a small, carefully laid out stone-lined path that trailed past a few manicured bushes and flowers. Over another small hill she spotted the first mausoleum carved into the shape of a tiny church, a cross reaching to the heavens from the top of the ornate granite. Stained glass windows decorated all four sides of the building. One depicted an olive branch, one a dove, one a chalice, and one a rising sun. The doors were chained shut; rust lined them, red creeping along the metal.

A few more carefully laid out gravestones scattered around the building with a bench laid out by a bed of flowers. "Someone comes to take care of these?" I motioned to the flowers.

"Yeah. The historical society has a gardener they hire to come out from time to time. I think every month or two," Jackson guessed. "The grass has been recently cut so I'm thinking they've been here in the last week."

I followed along the stone path past a few smaller buildings and a gravestone with a book closed carved into stone above the names of a family. I frowned when I spotted one mausoleum carved from a black stone that sat at the back of the cemetery. One of its doors hung faintly open.

"That looks promising," Aramis chimed in.

"Stay quiet, and stay here." I told him.

Jackson lingered behind me to take samples of some of the plants nearby and a few small samples of the dirt. She murmured to herself as she carefully labeled, bagged, and put away everything she collected.

I headed to the open mausoleum. "Look at this," I called to Jackson.

She finished bagging the last sample and hurried to my side.

"What mausoleum is this?" I asked.

Jackson shook her head. "I'm not sure. The name's worn off of the front here." She walked a slow circle around the building, running her hands over the rosemary bush beside the entrance. The building was simple, short without any windows and with no elaborate designs or carvings.

The doors were a basic iron, rusted with age though they moved easily enough as I tested one of them. It easily swung open with my touch.

I stepped into the mausoleum and looked around. I counted five small cubbies carved into the walls for bodies. Each had a casket carefully locked into place and held there. Plaques lined each shelf, though the names had long lost the battle with time, disappearing to the ravages of the ages. A single crack split through the granite floors running from the back to the front of the building.

Jackson stepped inside and let out a long breath before inhaling deeply.

"This has been disturbed recently," I murmured.

"What?" Jackson asked.

"There's hardly any dust in the air. If no one has been in here in years there should be some kind of dust or something to be disturbed by us." I frowned and took a deep breath.

Aramis stepped inside, "But who would be in here? There's nothing in here," Aramis asked. "How would this be useful at all?"

"I told you to wait outside." I snapped at Aramis.

He gave a faint smirk, "I got lonely."

I glared at him, but Jackson kept looking around.

"It does seem a bit small to serve as a super villain's home base, huh?" Jackson said.

I didn't respond as I ran my fingers along the edge of one of the shelves, tracing against the time worn plaque. It ran smooth and clean under my touch, no dust or pollen disturbed by my finger or by our presence in the mausoleum.

"They could've been in here for repairs or a burial. Maybe, someone's died recently," Jackson suggested.

I looked over my shoulder. "Then why are all the name plates faded? If someone was buried here a week or even a few months ago, the name plate wouldn't be faded away and there'd still be some kind of dust or something."

Aramis sighed, "Look, there's nothing in here but caskets and stones."

All three of us looked up when the door creaked closed. I reacted first, rushing to the door to try to get it open again but a distinctive sound of the of chains being dragged and tightened echoed throughout the crypt.

JACKSON RAN UP BESIDE me and began pounding on the door. "Hey! We're in here, open the doors!"

Aramis rammed his shoulder into the door. It budged only faintly but the sound of chains circling the door handles continued and then a lock clicked into place before clanking down against the door.

Jackson slammed her fist against the metal. "Hey!! Open it up!" She yelled.

I tried to force our only way out to open back up. The chains strained against the force as Jackson and Aramis joined in, pressing with all of their strength. A thin sliver of sunlight pierced into the room, but the chains forced the door closed again.

Jackson caught her breath. "Shit."

I focused on keeping my breathing steady as she looked around for anything I could use to pry the door open with.

Aramis looked at Jackson. "How frequently did you say those gardeners come here?"

Jackson laughed weakly. "If that wasn't them that just locked us in, then I don't know. It could be weeks before they come back." Jackson sank onto the floor, tugging at the ends of her hair.

I tried the door once more before pacing around the room, 6 steps long and 4 steps wide. I sighed and leaned against one of the caskets. It shifted under my weight, sliding further back. I frowned, pulling myself up on the shelf to look behind the casket, squinting against the darkness. I dragged a flashlight from my pack and shone it over the casket.

"There's something back here," I called, "Help me move this casket."

Jackson and Aramis slowly came to my side, each taking hold of one end of the old casket. The three of us carefully shifted it, shaking and sliding it free and off of the shelf. After we lowered it to the ground, I climbed on top of it to get a better look.

In the furthest backside of the shelf was a hole just big enough for one person leading straight down.

"Well, I guess this is it," I said, looking back at Aramis and Jackson.

"Is what?" Aramis asked.

"Our only way out," I said simply.

"I'll go first." I tied my bag firmly to my back. "Wait until you hear from me before you follow."

Jackson frowned, crossing her arms but relenting. "Alright, fine."

Aramis nodded. "And if we don't hear from you?"

I smiled. "Come after me anyways."

I held my flashlight firmly in my hand, checking my gun before sliding over to the hole. The flashlight's dim light only bounced off of steep rock edges but didn't show me the bottom. There's no other choice, so I took a deep breath before taking the final push and falling straight down.

I felt like I fell for hours, like Alice falling down the very wrong hole to Wonderland, flashes of bones and dirt briefly illuminated around. I hit a soft pile of cloth and rolled off of it quickly to look around the room.

Carved from dirt and crudely held up with posts, the room was barely high enough for me to not hit my head as I took perimeter. Nothing moved, and the only pathway I could see was a hallway leading off to my left side.

Something landed in the cloth beside me. I jumped backwards, drawing my gun, and only relaxing when my flashlight fell upon Jackson's face.

"I told you I would tell you when it was safe to jump!" I hissed.

"I got worried." Jackson brushed herself off and got to her feet. "This is under the cemetery. I had no idea anything like this even existed. Those legends about the Civil War tunnels under the cemetery were right."

"I don't think anyone knew for sure these existed." I frowned, moving toward the only hallway, shining my flashlight down it, not seeing anything.

A few seconds later Aramis crashed into the cloth and slid to his feet. I motioned for them to follow me and we started creeping down the hallway.

"Do we know what we're looking for?" Jackson asked.

I answered, "Well, we're looking for dead things trying to attack us or a crazed woman trying to kill us."

"Oh good," Jackson muttered. "Here I was worried about being overwhelmed by sunshine and rainbows."

The hallway continued, slowly winding and turning. "Any idea where it's leading us?" I asked.

Jackson pondered for a few moments. "Well, I think right now it's following under the stone path that leads through the rich section, and if that's the case we're heading back toward the mass grave section of the cemetery."

I nodded, ducking under a lower section of hallway, and sighed when it turned yet again.

"How long can this go? It's got to lead to somewhere," Aramis muttered.

"Doesn't mean it's somewhere we want to go," Jackson countered. "This could lead us to a big dead end for all we know."

I shook my head. "I doubt that."

Jackson sighed heavily, shifting her bag of supplies on her back before nodding. "I guess there really isn't any way but forward anyways, huh?" she said as she tucked some of her hair behind her ears.

I nodded, tossing the flashlight to Aramis. "Lead the way."

"Me?"

"You're the one who can 'feel' when the gem's close right?" I asked. "Help keep us on track. I bet this branches into different paths at some point and I'd rather stay on the one that's going to help us and not lead us to a blind stop. Or worse."

Aramis hesitated but finally relented, and began leading the way down the narrow tunnel. He kept the light focused straight ahead, flashlight in one hand, shovel clutched in the other. Jackson walked behind him and I kept up the rear, where I could keep an eye on Aramis and make sure nothing came at us from behind.

Every few steps, he would pause and look from side to side before continuing forward again. The path finally split into three separate directions: one curved sharply to the left, another continued straight ahead, and the third tilted downward deeper into the earth.

"Well?" I prodded when Aramis stood still and didn't make a move.

"I don't know," he admitted. "We're close. Very close, I can feel that, but I can't tell which way is the best way."

"Fat lot of good you are," I said.

"Let's just go about twenty feet down each of them, see if that helps you figure out which one is the best bet, ok?" Jackson suggested.

"Let's start with the left," I offered. Aramis hesitantly began down that path.

The tunnel narrowed until the loose dirt walls were crumbling around us and we had to turn back or risk being buried under tons of earth. Without another word, Aramis headed straight ahead into the darkness of the tunnel. The passage stayed wide as we continued walking forward.

Jackson took a deep breath. "I smell rosemary." She moved past Aramis.

He groaned and hurried after her, and I chased after the two.

"Look!" Jackson called, and I squinted, spotting a small patch of light. Following after Jackson, I saw a flat rock laid out over the earth; sunlight streamed in from the seams where stone met grass.

"This must be where they come in and out of the tunnels. Probably a grave stone or mausoleum." I said as I pushed at the stone above us.

It protested before finally budging and sliding off and falling to the side. Looking out, I immediately, noted I'd been right in my guess that this was a hidden grave hiding the path's exit. Obscured under a rosemary bush, the stone stayed out of the main view of the cemetery.

Jackson popped up beside me. "This is why they all have rosemary on them. They have to climb through this bush before they get anywhere."

"So we know where they're coming from exactly,"

Aramis said, staying in the tunnel, "But that doesn't help us find anything we came here for."

I nodded. "Come on, let's check the rest of these tunnels. One of them has to lead to her."

"It's always the last place you look," Jackson sighed.

"Because after you find it you stop looking," Aramis said, heading back down the tunnel.

I didn't pull the stone back into place as we all headed back down the tunnel. Better to leave it open to let the sunlight stream in so if we have to get out of here in a hurry, our escape is wide open. I ran my finger over the pistol against my hip and took a deep breath as Aramis led us on the march back the tunnels we'd investigated and to the fork in the path again. This time we turned down the untraveled path.

Sour, dirty clay choked the air keeping the tunnels firm enough though my shoes stuck to the ground, and my jeans would forever hold a rusty blood color from the thick Georgia clay clinging to my pants.

"Anything?" Jackson asked Aramis.

He closed his eyes, and held the flashlight still as he concentrated before he hesitantly nodded. "I think so."

Jackson pulled out her thermo-goggles and looked Aramis over. "Your chest is a little warmer," she said after a moment before pulling the goggles off and rubbing her eyes. "Guess that means we're getting closer, right?"

I nodded. "We've got to be. Keep going, Aramis."

He nodded, pointed the flashlight ahead, and continued creeping down the hallway. Suddenly, he froze and turned off the light.

"What are you doing!?" Jackson demanded.

"Shhh." Aramis hissed.

I pulled my pistol free from its holster and held it up. "I

hear them," I murmured. "How many?"

Aramis was silent before I heard him very quietly respond, "Six."

I nodded, and pushed Jackson behind me. "Stay here," I told her.

Aramis put the flashlight away and pulled the shovel from his back.

"You're just going to leave me here?" Jackson whispered.

"All of us rushing in is not going to lead to good things," I responded. "Now you stay here so we can find you again. Come on, Aramis."

Aramis took a deep breath and I briefly wondered if he still had to breathe or not. Shaking my head from that distraction, I crept down the dark tunnel toward the shifting shadows that lurched and tumbled forward.

I could hear them somewhat muttering under their breath, but nothing coherent. I tucked my pistol away; firing in tight quarters in total blackness wouldn't be a great idea. Pulling the knife from my holster, I let Aramis walk forward toward them.

7

A FEW GRUNTS AND THEN the solid thud of the shovel-head hitting something hard drifted back through the darkness. I waited a few moments until I felt something move past me and the scent of rot washed over me. I lurched the knife forwards into what I hoped was the juncture between the neck and chest and twisted.

Dust exploded under my fingers, flying all around me.

Another thud of the shovel sounded just to the left of me, and I ducked backwards, feeling the rush of air of the shovel swinging right by my head.

"Watch it, Aramis!" I growled.

"Behind you, Pulptress!" Jackson's voice called out and I ducked just in time to avoid something sharp piercing through my neck. It caught my hair, cutting through a few inches, but avoiding skin. I put my knife upwards into the groin of the creature behind me. It dropped to its knees and I grabbed for its head and twisted. Something snapped, then burst into dust.

Catching my breath I glanced toward Jackson's voice, "Any more?" I asked.

She paused before answering, "I don't see anything."

I put the knife away and let out a deep breath as I got back to my feet, "You don't listen very well, Doc."

"I don't do things that I know are bad ideas," Jackson countered. "And wandering off to fight things in the dark is not a good idea. So, how about my goggles and I take the lead from here on out?"

I frowned. "Just wear the goggles and follow behind Aramis. Keep an eye on his chest and see what the temperature change looks like. We need to follow after that and find this gem as soon as possible. That's priority right now."

"And after that?" Jackson asked.

"We find her and finish her once and for all," Aramis answered. "She will be looking for us. She has to know I'm here."

"Right, the gems react when they get close together." I sighed. "So let's move."

Aramis began back through the tunnel.

"How's she going to know it's your gem and not the one already here setting her gem off?" Jackson asked.

"The closer the three are, the stronger the sensation. Just being close to one other gem means some light but when the three get closer together, it's a heat," Aramis explained.

Jackson nodded. "So, there's no way of knowing if we're heading straight toward her or toward the missing gem."

I gripped the handle of my knife. "If we find her first, we'll deal with her and then find this thing and get rid of her for good."

Jackson sighed. "This was a terrible idea," she groaned.

"Too late to protest it now, you agreed, no, you insisted on coming."

"I know!" Jackson replied, then paused. "Temp in your chest is rising by a few degrees, Aramis. We're getting closer."

"I can tell. It's starting to burn," Aramis said. "Now, let's keep at it. Looks like it splits three ways up ahead again."

I groaned. "Jackson? Which way looks best?"

Jackson waited as Aramis walked a bit down every tunnel. "Right. The right made a huge jump in temperature almost immediately."

"Well then, lead the way. We've got to be getting close," I said, keeping up the rear as we started down the tunnel. The soft dirt walls closed in tightly around us, brushing against our shoulders with every step. The air was stagnant and sometimes difficult to breathe. Jackson suddenly stopped, "Okay, your chest is nearly at 98 degrees. It has to be close." She rustled through her bag and a flashlight flared to life.

I squinted against the sudden light and looked around.

Various bones jutted out from the walls, hanging in place around the narrow tunnel that appeared to end just a few feet from where we stood. "Looks like this is a section she hasn't really searched yet," Aramis said, rubbing his chest.

"Well, guess we better start looking around then." I knelt down, pulling a few bones loose of the dirt, and digging through some of the tunnel wall. After a few moments, Aramis and Jackson began searching as well.

"We don't have any kind of description to go on?" I asked as I dug through the dirt and bones around us.

"I already told you everything I know. It'll be small, probably smaller than a fist. It's going to be some kind of shade of grey, and it will be glowing since it's so close to me." Aramis said.

"Well glowing at least ought to be easy to identify," Jackson grumbled, pulling a bone loose from the wall and jumping back as dirt tumbled down. She sighed, kicking the dirt and bones free from her legs and getting back to digging.

Aramis stopped working. "Think we've got company." He raised the shovel.

I groaned and pulled my knife out again. To my left, I could see Jackson pulling a large bone from the wall and holding it up like a club. She frowned at me. "It's one of the hardest, strongest bones in the body."

"I know. It works pretty well," I said, remembering taking out quite a few chiffoniers in the catacombs of Paris with a leg bone as my only weapon.

The first one leapt from the darkness and was immediately caught by Aramis' shovel to the head. It crumbled into dust and then they began crawling out of the ground and walls.

One dove from overhead, crashing down on top of me and knocking me to the ground. My back slammed into the hard red clay and my breath rushed out of my body. I struggled to get my grip back solid on my knife, when suddenly there was a sharp crack and the monster pinning me was gone. Jackson offered me her free hand and helped pull me back to my feet. I nodded a wordless thanks and adjusted my knife in my hand.

Standing back to back with Jackson we turned slowly, taking out any of the creatures that rushed us or came too close to either one of us. We didn't work perfectly together, hitting one another with elbows as we swung and fought back, but that feeling of having someone at my back made the dark of the tunnel seem less terrifying.

Just out of the corner of my eye I saw Aramis with three of the creatures grabbing him. His shovel was bent at an odd angle, broken at his feet, and when Jackson's wildly swinging flashlight turned its beam toward that direction again, Aramis and the chiffoniers were gone.

8

I PULLED FROM JACKSON'S SIDE and rushed over to the broken shovel. My knife flew, ready to strike any creatures still rushing about, but now they all pushed down the hallway, away from Jackson and me.

"They took Aramis!" I slammed my fist into the wall, wincing at the hard red clay not giving an inch.

Jackson groaned, slowly getting to her feet. "Took him where?"

"To her," I growled, clenching my fist. "We need to get him back."

"What about finding the gem here?" Jackson asked. "It's got to be here."

"Without Aramis, we can't gauge that anymore. We don't want her to get him." I shook my head. "I'm not leaving him with her. I'm not losing anyone else to her."

Jackson was quiet before nodding. I heard her shuffling a bit through the dirt and bones, taking a deep breath before joining my side. Jackson followed after me, keeping the leg bone clutched in her hands, raised and at the ready.

"What are we going to do?" Jackson whispered.

"I'm going to put a bullet between her eyes, and we're

gonna get Aramis the hell out of there." I answered.

I quickened my pace. I could hear Jackson running right behind me, yelling for me and for Aramis. I kept the light from her flashlight just in my periphery vision as I continued down the winding, twisting dirt passageways. I only came to a stop when I hit in the fork in the paths and wavered on which way to go.

Jackson stumbled into me. "What are you doing?" she asked.

"Shine that light on the floor," I told her.

Jackson nodded and let the flashlight slowly sweep the ground. I knelt down low and carefully examined the moist earth. I could make out signs of a struggle and of someone being dragged. I pointed straight ahead and moved quickly down that hallway with Jackson right behind me. In the bouncing light of the flashlight I watched the trail continuing, turning left then right. Jackson struggled to keep up with me as I rushed through the hallways.

"Where are they taking him?" Jackson asked. "I didn't think these monsters would, you know, kidnap someone."

"They'll be taking him to their maker," I said. "She's probably had them looking for him specifically. He holds one of the gems that she needs, remember?"

Jackson nodded, jumping and dropping the light as something growled. The sound echoed around in the narrow tunnels. Jackson scrambled to get the flashlight back in her hand. "What was that?" she whispered.

"Turn off the light," I hissed.

Jackson fumbled with it but got the light off and pressed close against my side. I heard her fumble through her bag and then slide her goggles slide over her head and snap into place.

She took a sharp intake of breath. "We need to go. Now,"

she said.

"What do you see?" I asked.

"A lot of very big, very angry, likely very dead dogs. Those body temps I'm picking up are not compatible with life."

I looked around the darkness of the cave and finally saw the shine of something white and sharp. The growls grew louder and louder, starting to vibrate against the walls.

I took a deep breath and stepped backwards, pushing Jackson with me. We tiptoed a few tentative steps back when I heard paws slamming against the ground. I grabbed my flashlight from my belt, turning it on just in time to see a huge dog leaping toward me.

The matted fur hung in loose clumps from a skeletal body. Its skin pulled back tightly on its skull making the milky grey eyes look bigger, and the teeth stand out with a constant snarl. Pale green drool dripped from its jaw, and the one jumping towards us had the bones of its legs fully exposed.

I swung the flashlight and cracked it against the dead dog's skull. It dissolved to the ground.

Howls and growls began circling around us, and I felt Jackson tense behind me. "We're surrounded," she whispered.

"Take off your goggles, very slowly," I said softly, "and get your flashlight back out. Turn it on and duck."

"What?" She whispered back though I heard her going ahead and removing her goggles and putting them back into her bag. The batteries in her flashlight rattled softly as she pulled it back out.

"Ready?" I asked as I pulled my pistol out, and readied it. She took a deep breath. "Ready."

The flashlight burst to life, and light shone across the

hall around us. As Jackson ducked, I turned my pistol to fire several quick shots at the raised dead dogs that snarled at the edge of the light. Their bloodshot eyes stared at us, and most of them were missing their snout or ears, lost to rot and time.

I grabbed onto Jackson's wrist and took off past the stunned dogs. In an instant the chase was on, the pounding sound of the feet of the dogs hunting us down echoed all around as we fled through the twisting passages of the underground chamber.

Aramis' trail became long lost under the fleeing from the bloodthirsty creatures as Jackson and I ran as fast as we could. The light bounced in Jackson's grasp, flashing from wall to ceiling to pack of dogs and then back to our own feet. I turned and twisted through passages until the jumping beam of light hit something solid, something of stone, not dirt. I stopped and pulled Jackson toward it.

This area of the tunnel was not fully dug out, a large slab of rock blocking the passage.

"Keep your light on." I told Jackson as I shoved my flashlight back into my bag and tucked my pistol away.

Digging with my hands, I carved out a hole just big enough for me and Jackson to crawl behind the slab of stone. I pushed her in first and then climbed in after her, groaning in pain as one of the dog's feet caught my leg and tore through jeans and skin. I pushed in further, feeling the dog's teeth almost grazing me, snapping and clawing desperately as they began to dig to get to us.

"Now what?" Jackson asked.

I squinted into the darkness of the space around us, barely making out the gleam of something metal not far from us. "Come on." I crawled through the narrow space in the dirt, just barely big enough for me to fit.

Jackson shuffled behind me, coughing as dirt toppled around us. Behind us I could still hear the dogs snarling and clawing at the ground, trying to dig their way after us.

I nearly crawled into the shiny object and ran my hands over it, slowly tracing out the shape of a coffin. I frowned, but turned toward Jackson. "Help me move this. We can use it to barricade the hall so those dogs can't get to us."

Jackson crawled over to my side of the coffin, and together we pushed, starting to wedge the narrow coffin into the hallway just as I heard the dogs starting down the narrow passage towards us. The old metal creaked and groaned under our work. I heard the first dog hit the metal and growl with frustration, starting to claw and fight through the dirt.

I rammed my shoulder against the coffin and wedged it firmly in, jumping back when the metal creaked and then cracked. The side panel fell off, and in the dark, something slid onto the floor.

Jackson scrambled backwards, boots scraping the dirt. I heard her rustle through her bag before the flashlight clicked to life and swung wildly around until Jackson controlled herself and aimed the flashlight toward the coffin.

On the floor was the motionless body of a white haired man wearing what looked like an old Union civil war uniform. Around his neck was a bright gold medallion. His skeletal hand clasped tightly around the necklace. His skin had all but rotted away, exposing nothing but bone and tuffs of white hair along his head. His Confederate grey uniform hung in rags off of his bones. The skeleton still held together even though it should have fallen apart long ago.

Jackson gasped. "That's him. That's the devil my grandfather told me about."

9

"THE WHITE-HAIRED DEVIL ALWAYS had a pendant of gold! Always. They buried him alive and he just laughed and held onto his pendant until the ground ate him up." Jackson spoke in a hurried whisper, "It's just like grandfather told me."

I frowned, "That's a dead man with a necklace yes, but that doesn't make him—"

His hand clenched around the medallion and a slow wheeze of air escaped the rotted body. His head snapped toward us, nothing but hollow, empty space staring towards us.

I reached for my pistol, aiming squarely at an empty eye socket.

He took several slow deep breaths through his nose, sniffing the air. Then slowly, he began to drag himself toward us.

I fired straight through his skull. He slumped to the ground and I let out a breath I'd been holding. "Okay, we need to find a way that this connects back to the main tunnels," I told Jackson.

She nodded, and, with flashlight in hand, began crawling

forward through the dirt, I followed behind her.

I felt something circle around my ankle and then tug me sharply backwards, dragging my stomach against the ground as I struggled and kicked, glancing over my shoulder enough to see the tattered edges of a civil war uniform.

I kicked again and again until my free leg finally made contact with the corpse's jaw and he let go of me with a howl. In the tight space I struggled to aim again and fired at him, narrowly missing as the bullet slammed into the dirt wall beside me.

"Go!" I yelled at Jackson.

She scrambled forward and I crawled right behind her, glancing over my shoulder. I could hear the chains around the man's legs dragging against the dirt as he pulled himself after us and grabbed me again. This time he twisted, and I was just barely able to roll into the movement enough to keep him from snapping my ankle.

I kicked at him, struggling with the tight space and his firm grip around my ankle. He clawed up to my knee and began jerking me backwards, back toward the coffin. I heard Jackson yell something and then start after me.

"Let go!" I growled, managing to kick him hard enough to loosen his grip, but as we neared the coffin, the ceiling above raised slightly and he took that chance to leap onto me, pressing his hands around my throat and squeezing. I punched at him and kicked, rolling around and slamming him back into a coffin. He growled and lunged for me again, but Jackson was suddenly there with one of the handful of rosemary she'd collected in her hand. A lighter flicked to life and rosemary burst into flames as Jackson shoved the flaming sprig onto the man's uniform.

Instantly the cotton fabric was ablaze. The dead man howled and struggled, rolling from one side to the other, unable to put out the flames. I pulled my feet away from him and stared in stunned silence as the fire ate over him. As it slowly began to smolder out I looked to Jackson and asked, "How do you know that would stop him?"

"Granddaddy told me that they plant rosemary at the cemeteries to keep the devil away, and I knew those uniforms would be flammable," she said, catching her breath and coughing, trying to get the smoke out of her face.

I nodded, and paused as that glint of gold against his chest caught my eye again. I leaned in closer and reached over to it, pulling it off of his neck. He lunged forward to grab at my hands, but as soon as the necklace left his body, he crumbled into dust.

I took a slow breath and looked over the amulet in my head. One side was engraved with the image of a phoenix while the other side had a beautiful pale grey gem embedded in it.

"Do you really think that's it?" Jackson asked, leaning over my shoulder. "That man had it," she murmured. "The legends were true."

"Something is true," I muttered, turning the gem over in my hands, running my thumb over it and feeling the phoenix and the stone cold against my finger.

I winced when my leg burned from the dog's claws ripping into me. Jackson frowned. "Here, sit down for a second," she said.

Reluctantly I agreed, slowly sitting down on the ground, wincing and extending my leg out.

Jackson knelt beside me and tugged at her jacket. Pulling a pocketknife from her jacket, she carefully cut off the sleeve of her jacket and wrapped it tightly around my leg. She held pressure tightly against the wound, counting softly under her breath before tying it off. "We need to stop the bleeding before we get moving again," she said.

"We need to find Aramis," I responded, leaning against the wall and slowly getting back to my feet. "I've had worse. I'll be fine."

Jackson frowned, standing up after me. "I really think—"

"Look, we don't have time for this. We need to get to Aramis." I shook my head, and pulled out my flashlight and shone it around in a quick circle, finding a narrow pathway of loose dirt leading in a separate direction.

"Come on," I said before crawling forward down the pathway on my hands and knees.

Jackson sighed, but I heard her crawling steadily behind me. At several points, we had to stop and shove past a few loose clusters of dirt, digging our way forward.

I paused, Jackson nearly crawled into me. "What are you doing?" she grumbled.

"Just listen for a second," I hissed, closing my eyes. I could hear the dull thudding of feet against the ground, feel it vibrating overhead.

"I think we're below one of the tunnels," I said, opening my eyes. "Have you still got some weapon?" I asked.

Jackson nodded. "Yes." She pulled out a collapsible nightstick.

"Push it upwards through the roof here," I instructed.

"If I do that, it's gonna collapse down on us," Jackson protested.

"And we'll find the tunnel. Come on," I said. "Take a deep breath and do it."

Jackson hesitated and I could hear her turning the nightstick over and over in her hands before she took a sharp intake of breath. I did the same and waited.

The stick burst through the ceiling above us. Two chiffoniers and a pile of dirt collapsed on top of us. They hissed and immediately lunged at me. I pushed through the dirt and stabbed my knife firmly into one's neck. He dissolved into dust. As I turned toward the other one, Jackson burst through the dirt and cracked the bat against his skull. He toppled backwards into dust.

Coughing and spitting out dirt, Jackson crawled back out of the chaos and into the main tunnel. "That was the stupidest idea you've had," she muttered.

"So coming down here after a murderous necromancer wasn't the worst idea I've had?" I asked as I worked out of the dirt.

Jackson offered me her hand and helped get me to my feet. I winced a little before shaking off the pain in my leg. "Come on, we still have to find Aramis."

She frowned. "Lean on me," she offered.

"I'm fine," I insisted. I held the gem out in front of me and then turned the other way. It flickered with a soft grey glow. "This way then." I put the amulet around my neck.

"Is that leading us toward Aramis or toward that woman?" Jackson asked.

"I don't know," I admitted, "But unless you want to wander around in circles, this is the only direction we've got to go on." I held up the amulet as it flickered again.

"Alright, just be careful," Jackson said.

"Oh you know me. Always super careful." I smiled faintly as I continued down the hallway. Every few feet I held up the amulet. The flickering slowly strengthened each time, burning sharper against the metal and getting hot against my skin.

"Aramis?" Jackson called.

I put my hand to her mouth. "Shhh … Do you want more of those things to hear us?"

Jackson glared faintly but nodded and I slowly removed

my hand.

"Then how are we going to find him?" she asked.

I held the amulet up again. "This. This is all we have, so just trust me and we'll find him, alright?" I asked.

Reluctantly, Jackson slowly nodded.

I kept the lead, watching the gem carefully and letting it guide me through the tunnels, left and then right, and then straight ahead into total darkness. I tried to keep an eye out behind us, waiting for anything to jump out of the shadows and grab for us. But everything stayed still and totally silent. The quiet made my heart pound, wondering where all those things had gone. I wondered what the Bone Queen was now up to, but I tried to not let it worry me too much.

Pressing forward, the air use a different word than 'air' began to flow easier. Cool and crisp fresh air circulated around us and we both took a deep, slow breath in and slowly back out.

"Where's that coming from?" Jackson asked.

"I don't know, but let's keep going," I said, pushing forward toward the cool, crisp air.

We bumped into a solid slab of some sort of stone. Jackson and I worked together to push it to the side. I motioned for Jackson to stay down before I peered up, and found myself looking into a small church built into the tunnels. At the front of the church was a massive pit leading back down into the tunnels. I didn't see anything else around but a few empty, mostly rotted wooden pews. Wincing, I pulled myself up out of the ground and onto the floor. Jackson followed behind me.

"Where are we?" I whispered.

Jackson got out of the small coffin that led down into the pit, and brushed some of the dirt from her jeans. "I don't know," she said after a moment, taking a look around. "I'd guess a church."

"Really?" I sighed. "That's obvious. Are we still in the cemetery?"

Jackson nodded. "I guess this could be an old church somewhere out there. There's acres of land and at least one church. Judging by the state of the wood that the pews are made out of, that'd be the best guess I have, but as for geographically 'where are we?'" She shook her head. "I'm sorry, but I don't have a clue."

"But we're still close to the Bone Queen." I said.

"Or Aramis," she added, pointing to the gem around my neck. In the dim light of the church, its glow was pronounced, reflecting against the dark of my shirt.

"And I'd say we're getting closer," I said. "Let's take a look around then. Stay close."

Jackson nodded and kept right at my side. I stepped carefully, the floor worn away to bare dirt in many places, though a few still had patches of wood that creaked and groaned when any kind of weight was put on them.

An altar at the front of the room was decorated with skulls and other bones displayed out by a chalice and a mirror. I shook my head as I walked over to the items. "She's been here."

"This is where she summons those things," Jackson guessed. "She brings the bones here and raises them here, gives them instructions and then," she pointed back toward the coffin that led to the tunnels they'd just crawled out of, "then she sends them out that way."

I nodded. "That sounds logical. But why bring the bones here when she could just summon them straight from the ground?"

"I don't think those tunnels were always here," Jackson

said. "What if she had to summon help to look for that stone? She started here and worked outwards through the rest of the cemetery."

"She doesn't know where it is either," I muttered. "She has as much of a clue as Aramis did."

"She might have known a bit more than I did," Aramis' voice spoke up.

10

J ACKSON JUMPED AND GRABBED my arm as I immediately
drew my pistol and raised it. I took quick stock of the
empty spaces around the church, but there was no sign
of Aramis.

Jackson gasped and I looked up to find Aramis sus-
pended from the ceiling with thick wires tied around his
arms. Parts of his skin were ripped open, exposing the
hollow parts of his chest.

"We'll get you down," Jackson promised, and started
looking for the way up to the ceiling.

"Over here!" I called, spotting an old, ragged ladder. I
put my gun away before grabbing the ladder. Jackson helped
me get it planted and then started trying to climb up it.

"No, let me. I've got better balance." I pushed Jackson
out of the way and slowly began making my way up the
ladder as it started to rock. Jackson rushed over and held
it steady. I nodded thanks as I slowly ascended toward the
trapped man.

"She tried to get the gem from me," he said.

"And?" I asked, pulling out my knife.

"She couldn't quite manage to cut it out." He laughed.

"Finally just said she'd use me to find it."

"What?" I froze, knife just above the top holding him up. "This is a trap."

"What did you think it was?" Aramis sighed.

Growling, I slashed at the rope, and he plummeted to the church floor, landing on two chiffoniers that rushed in from the tunnels. The ladder rocked again, but Jackson held it steady, kicking at the creatures that came close to her. More creatures rushed into the church all of them crowded around us.

I rushed down several rungs before launching myself off the ladder and into the closest creature. I plowed my knife straight into its eye, and then rolled across the floor, popping up with my gun in hand.

Jackson rushed over to Aramis' side, shaking him as he groaned. "Aramis! Hurry up!"

She shook him harder as more creatures appeared and started toward her. My first bullet tore through three of the rag and bone men and sent them crumpling into dust onto the floor. Jackson pulled Aramis to his feet. His head slumped to the side, and his feet curled under him, but he tried to help get himself upright.

I hurried over and tried to steady him, firing off a few more rounds, trying to find a way out. "If there's a way in there's got to be another way out. Where are they coming from?" I muttered out loud.

A large boom shook the ground, and I watched as the largest man zombie I'd ever seen climbed from a pit in the ground. He looked at me and screeched.

I fired immediately, but the bullet striking his chest barely slowed him as he rushed for me. I shoved Jackson and Aramis out of the way just as the huge creature plowed into me and tackled me to the ground.

My gun flew out of my hand. I scrambled to grab my dagger and, drawing it, slashed across the inside of his thighs. He howled and slammed his fist at my head. I barely dodged out of the way as a rush of air flew past me.

He reared his fist back again and one meaty hand clenched around my throat. I chocked and struggled, kicking and stabbing at his thick arm, but his grip only tightened. My vision started going black when I heard a sharp pop and red dust suddenly poured over me.

Sitting up, coughing I spotted Jackson standing behind where the massive monster had been, gun still in the air where the man's head would have been. Her shoulders raised and fell in rapid succession as she tried to catch her breath.

"Come on, this way!" Aramis called, motioning to a small side door.

I grabbed Jackson and pulled her after me as I rushed for him. I paused only long enough to snatch my pistol from the floor before the three of us pushed through the door and Aramis barricaded it behind us. The creatures screamed and clawed at the thick wooden door but despite its groans of protest, the door held firm and steady against the onslaught.

I took a quick look around the room, a bare bones crypt, obviously vandalized and stripped bare. "Great. Now what?" I glared at Aramis.

"There's a hidden passage out of here," Aramis moved over to one of the coffins, and began to press against the loose stone, eventually one clicked and I heard something vibrate and scrape against the hard stone. A thin door opened on the opposite side of the room.

"And how did you know about that?" Jackson asked.

"This is the way they brought me in. She's this way," he said slowly.

I took a deep breath, and reloaded my pistol. "Well, let's go say hello and thank her for her hospitality."

"Why don't you wait here?" Aramis offered Jackson.

I nodded and added, "This doesn't have anything to do with you. You've got more than enough to prove your case to your boss."

"I'm not just gonna sit here and wait for either those things to kill me or to waste away down here on my own. No, I've come this far," she swallowed hard, "I want to see this through. Besides, I still don't have any proof about her bringing dead things back to life. That's the lynchpin of this case."

"You're still worried about proving to your boss that you didn't lose those bodies?" I asked.

Jackson smiled weakly. "I figure this is my only chance to get out and have an adventure like this. When I was little I always wanted to be some kind of hero and, well, I've got the chance. I'm not just going to walk away from that."

I shook my head. "Well, just try to stay out of the way. We've just got to get her sword from her."

Aramis glanced at the necklace around my neck. "It really was here. I guess it made a new home once it left France." He shook his head. "I tried to follow it, but once it left France it was harder to know where to look. The family I gave it to mostly died during the revolution. A few escaped and I bet sold whatever jewelry they had to make a new life. She must have followed it too somehow."

"Let's not keep her waiting then. I think you both have been waiting a long time for this," I said as I loaded my pistol. "Lead the way, Aramis."

He nodded and headed into the hidden doorway. Jackson walked close at his heels and I followed in the back.

These halls were cleaner and sturdier than the ones we'd

just left, lined with stone, and braced to hold steady. The work looked more recent than the interior of the church. I could see dozens and dozens of footprints embedded in the clay leading back toward the church.

"So who was she to you?" Jackson asked.

"Who?" Aramis responded.

"This Bone Queen. You knew her."

He sighed. "I thought I did," he said. "I was young, and she ... well, she was the most beautiful, dangerous, incredible woman I'd ever seen." He shook his head. "She was passionate about death, devoted to her god, willing to die for it, but she lost her way. And I ... well, I didn't step in to try to help her until it was too late."

"Is that why you keep it in your chest?" Jackson asked.

He sighed again. "I keep it there because it's safer that way."

"Wouldn't it be safest in a desert or at the bottom of the ocean?" Jackson countered.

"I kept it because I want to stop this, to stop her. She was never supposed to be like this, and, it's too late, but I want to free her," he said.

"How very noble of you," I commented. "We're getting closer now, right? Look at how much it's glowing." I pointed to the necklace.

"She keeps her quarters up here," Aramis nodded.

"She took you to her room?" I asked.

Aramis shook his head. "No, but I know her. She would keep her room at the heart of her work. She'll be rising by now, and she'll know we're coming."

"Good. Then we won't have to worry about introductions," I said.

11

JACKSON SWALLOWED AGAIN, WRINGING her hands together as we stepped into another section of hallway with a door at the end of it.

I crept down the hallway, one hand on my pistol. Blood dripped down my leg from the dog's claw marks, the gashes pulling open at some point in the last few fights. I tried to ignore the pain and not limp. There wasn't time to stop and tend to something that wasn't life threatening, not with the Bone Queen so close.

"You're bleeding again." Jackson touched my shoulder.

I jerked and nearly elbowed her, but just barely caught myself. "It's nothing," I insisted.

"With all these dead bodies and dirt around it is a big deal," Jackson said. "Do you know what kind of bacteria or infection could get into an open wound like that? Sit down," she ordered.

Aramis shifted on his feet, glancing toward the door. "I don't think—"

"Another minute isn't going to change anything," Jackson snapped. "And I'd rather have someone not bleeding through a fight. We need everyone at their best, right? Who

83

know what she might throw at us so we'd best be prepared."
Jackson nodded to herself.

I grunted in pain when Jackson exposed the wound.
She tsked at the blood-soaked jacket and began carefully
removing it. She pulled a few things from her bag. I watched
her set out a few strips of gauze, some type of ointment,
and some alcohol.

I started to protest. "I don't need—"

"You're gonna let me take care of this." Jackson glared.

I opened my mouth to tell her to knock it off, but then
she poured some alcohol onto a rag and began slowly
cleaning the wound. My protests were swallowed up as
the alcohol hissed and bubbled against my skin. Pulling on
a pair of gloves, she carefully began to apply the ointment
over the wound, frowning at the deepness of it, and mum-
bling under her breath. She wrapped gauze all around my
leg, tying it around me firmly, then taping it in place. She
tested the tightness and nodded. "I think that's the best
I can do out here, but once we get out of here you really
ought to go the hospital. I think you might need stitches
or staples or something. That wound is—"

"Thanks, Jackson." I cautiously tested the mobility of
my leg. While the wound stung and hurt, it no longer
burned through my body and took over all my other senses.
I nodded at her. "That'll be fine till we finish here, then I'll
head to a hospital, deal?" I asked.

Jackson sighed heavily as she picked up all her trash
and tucked it into a bag, "Fine. But I still think you need
stitches now."

"Well, more than likely I'm going to get banged up in
this fight, so hey, two for one hospital visit right?" I offered
with a grin.

"If you girls are done, we should get going," Aramis

said, arms crossed over his chest, leaning against the wall. His hand drummed a beat over his heart, and I could just barely make out a spark of light under his skin.

The gem around my neck glimmered. We had to be very close. I glanced back toward the door at the end of the hallway and rolled my shoulders, adjusting my pistol in my hand and checking my rounds once again. Full chambers and ready to roll.

I nodded to Aramis and Jackson. Aramis stepped back behind me, and Jackson ducked behind him.

Tiptoeing down the hallways toward the door, I could hear Amaury's voice echoing in my head, could see him, see his twisted risen from the dead skeleton rushing toward me with murder and nothing else in his eyes as I was forced to kill him in Paris. I took a deep breath and tightened my grip on the pistol. I was going to make her pay for what she did to him, for what she'd done to everyone over the ages, but if I was honest, I just wanted her to suffer and feel like Amaury had before his death.

I paused at the door and held my breath to listen and see what lurched behind. I closed my eyes and strained to hear anything. Nothing stirred behind the door. If she was here, she was still and silent as the grave.

Aramis looked at me and motioned to the door. I nodded and carefully tried the handle, surprised when it easily swung open. I took a deep breath and burst into the room.

Shadows twisted in every corner against the only light in the room, an old oil lantern hanging from the ceiling and swinging slowly. From the glimpses of light I could see what looked like a bedroom. A dresser with fine combs and a mirror stood closest to the door. A small bed was in the opposite corner, blankets a mess and kicked to the side.

I frowned. "Where are you?" I finally yelled. "It's over!"

Laughter answered me.
Behind me, I heard Aramis scream.

12

URNING AND TRYING TO catch a glimpse in the light, I
barely caught sight of a sword ripping through Aramis'
chest. The man clawed at the faceless person behind
him, but couldn't reach anything. I fired toward the sword,
and the sword and figure withdrew from Aramis.

He coughed and hit the ground. Jackson dropped down
to his side, trying to hold pressure against the wound even
though no blood flowed from the gaping hole.

"You should know better than to keep following me,
Aramis. I thought you had learned your lesson years ago."

I recognized the voice instantly as the Bone Queen's.

She laughed. "But here you are, still chasing after me."

"Renata. This isn't what you wanted. You were trying to
stop the plague, remember?" Aramis choked out, shakily
trying to get back to his feet.

She snorted, "See, even then you didn't understand,
Aramis. Even before I had this power you didn't understand.
I never wanted to stop the plague."

"What?" Aramis struggled to look up.

"I wanted to stop the dead rising again, not stop people
from dying. Death is the only inevitable, is the only truth

in this world of lies and disguises," she continued, and I felt something cold as a ghost by my side.

Turning, I fired and heard the bullet hit something then clink to the ground.

"You're a better shot than I remember, Pulptress." The Bone Queen laughed.

"Renata, stop this!" Aramis called. "Our time is over. You have to know that."

"Oh, dear sweet Aramis. You never understood; you never wanted to understand," she said. "The only thing I believe in, the only thing that I belong with is death. I know you believe that you can save me, but I don't want to be rescued. I want to drown this world in death. When no one but the dead are left, there will be nothing left to worship but death."

"That isn't what you really believe!" Aramis argued.

"You don't know what I really believe," The Bone Queen growled.

Aramis pushed Jackson to the side as the sword ruptured through his chest again.

Aramis grabbed at the sword, the blade slicing into his fingers as he pulled the blade further into his body until finally, the hilt was flush against his chest and the Bone Queen appeared in the light.

Her dark hair was matted, and her pale flesh had rotted further away to expose bone and hollowness under the skin. One eye was nothing but an empty socket surrounded by bone, and her jaw was partially exposed, hanging open in a gaping maw. Aramis looked over his shoulder at her, "I told you I would follow you anywhere," he said softly.

"And you've done a fine job." Her mouth twisted into something that might have been a smile. "Collected all three gems for me, too."

Something cracked and the Bone Queen tumbled backwards, and I caught a glance of Jackson, nightstick held high, and ready for another swing. I took the moment to fire several shots, listening to the thud of them ripping through the Queen's hollow body.

She laughed as the bullet-riddled body dropped to the ground and faded into dust. I took a step closer, and a raven burst from the dust and flew straight at me. Clawing across my face, its beak snapped at the necklace I wore, ripping it off of me and swallowing the glittering treasure.

As I rushed after the raven, I crashed into a large rotted corpse. Jackson swung the nightstick again, cracking into its skull, and suddenly dozens more bodies began crawling from the ground towards us. I glanced at Aramis and Jackson; the three of us moved closer together, forming a circle as the creatures descended. I could hear the swinging of Jackson's baton, and Aramis' daggers cutting through paper-thin skin and bone, but my attention was on keeping my guns loaded and firing. The smell of sulfur burnt around me, a faint layer of smoke and kicked up dust and dirt filtering through the air.

When stillness finally returned to the world, I caught my breath. For a few moments, I didn't think I could tell up from down. Slowly the world stabilized and I could see Jackson saying something, but couldn't hear a word.

I shook my head a few times, and finally could hear Aramis.

The sword in Aramis' chest dissolved away to dust and he brushed himself off, coughing as he felt over his body. In the now exposed hollows of his chest I could see the glint of the gem flickering against the emptiness of his long dead body. He adjusted his shirt to hide the gaping wounds.

"We need to go after her!" He yelled.

I nodded, and let Aramis take the lead. We ran down the hallway. "She's got the damned stone!" Aramis growled.

"We're in trouble," Jackson said.

Aramis laughed. "We're in an underground labyrinth being pursued by undead monsters while we hunt down their queen. I don't think there's any way this could not be considered 'in trouble'."

I shook my head with a faint smile; he had a point.

"How's your leg?" Jackson asked me.

"Fine," I answered without considering the question. If I didn't think about it, I didn't notice the pain surging through my leg with every step. "Do you know where we're headed?" I called to Aramis.

"No," He admitted. "But there's only one hallway leading from that room, so …"

"Here we are," Jackson finished, keeping pace behind Aramis, and just a few steps in front of me.

I heard something under us click, and the ground shook beneath our feet. I saw Jackson start to fall downwards and grabbed for her. She wrapped her hand around my wrist as all three of us began to plummet down through the trap doors that had just opened beneath us.

13

FEELING A LITTLE LIKE Alice falling into Wonderland, I wondered if the darkness I tumbled through would ever end. Aramis fell below me. I couldn't quite see him but I could hear him yelling occasionally.

I spread my arms and legs wide to slow my fall. My fingers grazed against the sides of the dirt tunnel, and I tried to claw at anything, but the few roots I managed to grab onto only jerked loose and offered no help. Jackson mimicked my movements, panicking as she struggled to grab onto anything to slow herself.

Out of the corner of my eye I saw Aramis straighten out his body to land on his feet. I heard the sharp crack of him hitting the ground and tried to brace myself. I tilted vertically and landed hard on my feet, then rolled to the side with my arms tucked up over my head.

I heard Jackson hit something softer than the ground and then Aramis groan in pain.

I scrambled back upright, ignoring the jolt of pain that shot up my leg and nearly stole my breath. "Aramis? Jackson?" I called.

For several seconds, no one responded, then slowly, "You

okay?" Jackson asked quietly.

"Peachy," Aramis muttered.

I followed their voices and found Jackson crawling off of Aramis, who appeared to have helped break Jackson's fall. His leg was twisted and broken, and a few shards of ribs pierced through his shirt. He sighed, and winced when Jackson immediately set about getting them back in place.

"It's fine," he grumbled.

She shushed him and quickly pushed everything back into place.

I said, "We need you moving."

Aramis just grunted as his bones slowly shifted back where they belonged. He let out a deep breath. "Everyone else okay?"

Jackson nodded. "Thanks to you." She offered a smile.

"Oh, having a lovely woman fall on me is always my pleasure," Aramis said with a wink.

Jackson swatted his shoulder.

"Come on, we need to move, we've got to find her," I said, pushing ahead to look around.

The room we'd dropped into appeared to be a small pit with no doorways leading in or out. I watched Aramis pace the room, noticing that when he approached the north wall, the gem exposed in his chest flickered to life with a burst of grey light.

I looked at the wall, running my hands over it.

"I think you need to sit down," Jackson touched my shoulder.

"I'm fine," I responded automatically.

Jackson sighed. "You've lost a lot of blood, and that leg. I'm worried that—"

"Look, worry all you want, but there isn't a hospital down here and in case you haven't noticed, it's too late to turn back." I took a deep breath, "Thank you for your help, but until we get out of here, and destroy these stones and her, then we're not going anywhere."

Jackson nodded, "I know, but … I just don't know how you're even upright right now, most people would be—"

"I'm not most people, and I've had worse. Promise, I'll be fine just as soon as we're out of here."

Jackson was quiet again before quietly asking, "If these stones keep Aramis alive … do you think it could heal you?"

"What?" I froze mid-step.

"What?" Aramis said, turning to face her.

"I'm just saying. That stone in your chest is keeping you alive, Aramis, and now we've got it, what if it could heal you, Pulptress? You're still bleeding, you could die."

"I'm not using anything involved with that damned woman for any reason," I growled. "No. I will drop dead before I let her magic keep me alive and walking around."

"No. Let that stone touch you and that'll be the end of you." Aramis shook his head.

"You're still here." Jackson argued.

"That doesn't mean you won't turn into something you don't like if you try to use that as a heal all." Jackson said, "I've seen it happen."

"You're still you." Jackson protested.

"And I fight every second to keep it." Aramis snapped. "You can hear her calling for you all the time." He shook his head. "No. There is no good use to these damned things."

"Are you sure?" Jackson asked. "It could—"

"No, and that's final!" I shouted at Jackson.

She flinched backwards, but didn't argue with me again.

14

RAMIS TOOK A FEW deep breaths before he began pushing his fingers into the dark wall where his gem glowed the brightest. After a few seconds he was able to push his hand through the wall. He frowned and pulled back.

"I can feel an open space behind this wall," he explained.

I pushed my arm through the wall and after getting elbow deep into the dirt, my hand burst free on the other side and grasped at the air. "Help me clear this space," I said.

Jackson and Aramis moved quickly and the three of us began digging with our hands through the dirt packed wall. Within a few moments, the dirt crumbled away to reveal a narrow hallway.

I didn't wait before starting down the hall. She'd made a fool of me ripping the stone from me like I was a pathetic baby. I clenched my fists. I would stop her no matter what.

Aramis and Jackson stayed right at my heels.

We turned a corner and a sharp beam of light pierced the darkness. Instinctively, I threw a hand over my eyes.

"Okay, tell me you see that light at the end of the tunnel too?" Aramis said.

"Yeah. Yeah, I see it. Is that daylight?" Jackson asked.

"Somehow I doubt that," I said. "It's probably a trap of some sort."

I closed my eyes for a moment and just listened, hearing the distinct scratching of metal against stone.

"Stay back," I said.

Aramis frowned at me. "You're hurt," he reminded me.

"I am aware." I grunted.

"Let me look first at least," he offered, and stepped toward the light before I could stop him. I waited only a second before going after him. Behind me, I heard Jackson curse, then follow after me.

Aramis stepped into the light, and I heard him take a sharp gasp of air. I rushed in, gun at the ready.

A man I hadn't seen before stood up. He wore a long black robe and his head was covered in pale blond hair that lingered down and looped around his chin into a beard. Most of his teeth were missing and his skin sunk, pale and yellow against his bones. He gave me a toothless grin as he pulled his sword from its hilt. "Ah, the Pulptress. I see you still keep good company, Aramis."

"Been expecting us, I take it?" I asked, carefully stepping into the room, keeping a safe distance from the tall, thin man as I made my way to Aramis' side.

"I've been waiting quite a while for you to get here," he confirmed as he held his sword at his side and shifted his weight from side to side on his feet.

"So sorry to make you wait, I hate being late," I said taking a slow step forward and raising my pistol.

"Going to shoot me where I stand?" he asked, still smiling.

"Why wouldn't I?" I replied, aiming between his eyes.

"Don't." Aramis put his hand over mine and slowly

lowered my gun.

The man grinned again. "So you do still have some sense left, Aramis."

"More than you," Aramis said. "What are you doing here, Eten? I thought you were long dead and gone."

"I was, but she has a way of bringing you back, doesn't she?" he asked, looking down at his hands where the skin had started to peel back from his bones.

"Give me one good reason why I shouldn't blow him to kingdom come right this second," I demanded of either man.

"Because I'm the best chance you have of finding what you're looking for." His grin widened as he spoke. "You're trying to find her, trying to kill her, trying to stop death."

"And you're working for her," I said, keeping my gun ready.

"And I know where she is," he said simply, scraping his sword across the ground. Sparks jumped from the blade to the stone floor before flickering out again.

"And you're just going to tell us?" Jackson finally spoke up, peering out from behind me.

He laughed. "Oh no. She's told me all about you, Pulptress. All about how you stopped her in Paris."

"More like slowed her down it seems," I muttered, tightening my grip on my pistol, feeling the tension of the trigger under my finger. "Get to the point, dead man walking."

"If you shoot me, I'll fade to dust without telling you a thing," he said.

"And what? If I let you go, you'll tell me what I want to know?" I shook my head. "That's not happening."

"Eten, be reasonable," Aramis started, but stopped when the man raised his hand.

"I don't want you to let me go," he said after a few

moments and looked to me. "I want a burial."

I frowned. "You want a what?"

"I want a proper burial. I never got one in life. I died and was raised again to be at her side, and then my bones were lost to time. She found me and raised me again, but all I want to be is put to rest," he said.

Jackson looked between me and Eten, "If we kill you, you'll fade to dust and—"

"And to the bone she raised me from. I want that bone buried. I want a plot of land to rest, a headstone. I want to be remembered."

I frowned. "That's all you want? A funeral and grave?"

"I'm a simple man. Or I was," he said with a sigh, and a weak laugh. "We both once were simple men, weren't we, Aramis?"

Aramis didn't respond, but stepped closer to the man. "What has she done?" he asked softly.

"I tried to stop her, but I couldn't, and even now I'm still powerless to stop her from the path she is set upon. I was supposed to lead but I can't stop her. Now, I just want to rest, and to meet death. I think the goddess of death is the only one who can stop her from this path she has set herself upon." He stood up to his full height, sword in hand, and at the ready.

I tensed and raised my gun again.

"We're going to stop her," Aramis promised. "I know in life we never were friends, but now," Aramis looked down at the exposed pit of his chest, "but now—"

"We are brothers." Eten nodded. "Useless brothers bound to the same woman." He shook his head.

"We'll bury you," Jackson said, stepping forward. "I promise. When this is all over, I'll bury you. I'll even come bring you flowers."

Eten smiled faintly, a gapping toothless smile. "You are a dear sweet child." He looked at me. "And you. You are touched by death, painted by it. Who is to say you are not acting as the hand of the goddess to stop her fallen child?"

"I'm no one's puppet," I growled, bristling at the very thought.

He tilted his head. "I can see the touch of Mene upon you. Though you do not carry her gem now, it still taints you just as it taints my lady."

"I'm not her," I snarled, curling my hand tighter around the pistol and taking a deep breath. "I'm nothing at all like her."

He smiled. "You are more like her than you'd care to admit." He closed his eyes and let out a heavy sigh. "But that is neither here nor there. If you stop her, then you have fulfilled the will of Mene and of death. Stop her." He opened his eyes and looked at Jackson. "You swear you will bury me?"

Jackson didn't hesitate. "Yeah. I'll get you a real plot with a headstone and everything, promise."

He smiled again, this time his lips stretching wider across his face. "Thank you."

"Tell me where she is," I demanded. "That's your end of the bargain, right?"

He nodded. "Of course." He took a slow deep breath, then said, "She continues down this path into a room that is locked. I finished the old tunnels already here, and built new ones to let her rag and bone warriors wander. I helped her raise these dead for her then was left to guard her. The lock that leads to her will only open with my sword as its key. Use my blade to unlock the door at the end of this tunnel. Leave the sword and continue down the stairs there. She will be at the altar at the bottom with the stones she has."

"She's waiting for us?" Aramis asked.

He shrugged. "She always waits for those gems to return to her, it's all she knows anymore. Living dead is not a sustainable life."

Aramis nodded, reaching out and taking Eten's hand. The two men embraced, patting one another's back before drawing apart. "Make it a clean shot," Aramis told me.

"Thank you, Pulptress." Eten closed his eyes and bowed his head.

I aimed carefully and fired. The bullet cracked through his skull just between his eyes. His eyes flew open for just a moment before his pale, dirty skin faded away and he dissolved into dust that floated across the air before dissipating. All that was left behind was a fragment of skull just in front of my feet. I tucked my pistol away and wiped my hands off on my jeans.

Jackson picked up the skull fragment, putting it into her back pocket.

"Are you alright?" Jackson asked Aramis.

He took a deep breath. "I'll be alright." He forced a smile. "Eten was a good man. Twisted in his own ways, but he didn't deserve this. None of us did." He let out his breath. "Come on."

I picked up Eten's sword and headed down the only hallway available to us. Torches flared to life as we walked down the hallway. "Guess there's no doubt she knows we're coming." I muttered.

Aramis nodded. "Well the glowing stones really don't do well for sneak attacks."

"So who was he?" Jackson asked after several moments of silence.

Aramis sighed deeply, "He was a priest of the goddess Mene, the same goddess that the Bone Queen once worshipped. Of course, she was still Renata back then. They traveled together as a part of the same group, and I was with them for a time at the end. Ultimately, they all fell to death or to Renata's own purpose."

My steps were steadier now as I walked past the few bits of remaining dust, kicking them up under foot and sending the pale yellow powder flying through the air again. Jackson hurried close behind, waving her hand in front of her face to try to keep the dust away.

"Do you think she knew he would do that?" Jackson asked.

"Who?" I said absently, trying to see what lay ahead down the hallway.

"Eten. Do you think she knew he would give us the key to her?"

Aramis answered, "I think she did. She needs us to get the last gem. Well, she needs me."

"So, we're walking right into whatever trap she's set for us," Jackson muttered.

"And we'll be ready for her," I promised.

A door led out of one hallway and into another narrow hallway that ended in a set of stairs curling downwards. At the very bottom of the steps that curled round and round, we found a locked door.

Jackson raised her bat and Aramis readied his daggers as I pushed the sword into the keyhole. Something mechanical whirred and clicked, bits of dust flew out of the slot around the sword before something grabbed the sword and jerked it forward into the door. The sword handle clicked into place flush against the door. I slowly gripped the handle and turned. The door swung open into a room draped with red crushed velvet.

In the center of the room stood an altar draped with

black fabric, candles burned all the way down, nearly to the point of burning themselves out. A few feathers and bones laid scattered across the table surface along with a short ceremonial knife with a blade blunted by time and wear.

"What is this?" Jackson whispered beside me.

I shook my head. "I think this is the end of the line." I looked around the room. Hanging on several of the walls were strange pieces of art decayed from time. The floor beneath our feet was littered with bones and each step sent the pieces of skeletons scattering across the ground beneath our feet.

I could hear Jackson's slow, shaky in and out breaths as she followed right behind me, not faltering or hesitating.

"Renata!" Aramis shouted.

"Come on out, we both know it's over," I called as I brought my pistol into my hand. "I know you're in here, and the time's over for this whole cat and mouse thing. You're caught."

"Am I the one caught or am I the one who has caught you?" Her voice echoed across the room.

Jackson jumped, tightening her grip on her bat.

"We're ready for you," I said, standing up straight and keeping my voice firm as I looked around the room, finally spotting the glint of light against the far back.

The pale grey light that flickered there matched the light from the gem that the raven had stolen from me. Without waiting, I turned my pistol, aimed, and fired toward the light.

Metal burned through bone and then hit stone. In the next instant, I saw a flash of light surging toward us. I grabbed Jackson's shoulder and pushed her out of the way. Aramis dropped to the ground just barely dodging the flare of metal flying across the space where he'd just stood.

Jackson hit the ground and crawled away while I fired toward the woman made of nothing but bone and scraps of fabric and skin. She glared toward me, half her skull gone, and the remaining sheets of her dark hair billowing around the empty space. Turning toward me I watched her skull slowly rebuild itself, stitching new pieces of bone together and slowly reforming what my bullet had torn through.

"Nice shot," she said, holding her sword in hand, gem handle glimmering.

"See, last time we didn't get a fair fight. You caught me without any of my guns," I said as I stepped in front of Jackson. "And, as I recall, you ran before we could finish our little spat. I think it's time we picked it back up."

She frowned, walking in a slow circle around Jackson and me, but I kept myself between her and Aramis. "If you want that stone you have to go through me," I said calmly.

"I suppose we both knew it would come to this eventually," she mused, "Ever since I first saw you hunting through the catacombs of Paris, I knew it would come to this. I knew that death would come for you and I would be her weapon once again."

"Don't flatter yourself," I said. "You're no one's weapon. You're doing this for yourself, and I'm here to do what I always do: stop the monster and save the day." I grinned. "It's a tough job but what can I say? I'm good at what I do."

"Renata, please! It's time to let go. No one is meant to live forever. You use to believe that. Please," Aramis begged.

She glared, growling low in her throat before she lunged at me.

I dodged the attack, though the blade just grazed my arm, barely slicing through the remaining fabric of my shirt enough for a thin cut to begin to ooze.

"Frightened of your death?" She asked me.

I shrugged. "I'm not frightened of you."

"Then you are as big a fool as I always thought," she sneered, lifting her sword and adjusting the hilt in her hands to let her thumb trace over the gem in the handle.

I noticed the skin along her arms and hand peeled back in thin sheets, exposing pale, thin bone beneath the surface. I could see straight into her chest cavity through the opening in her ribs just above where her belly button would have been if she still had skin. The stolen necklace glimmered against her empty chest cavity.

Looking down toward her feet, I realized she was missing one shoe and only a bare skeleton foot was visible just below the billowing of her cape swirling around her.

"You look like you're falling apart," I said, taking a careful step back, gently guiding Jackson and Aramis toward the door we'd entered from.

I felt Jackson hesitate, but then she rushed back toward the door. The Bone Queen lunged after her, but Aramis blocked her. The two undead clashed together, their swords interlocking, until the Bone Queen forced Aramis to his knees.

Jackson screamed as the Bone Queen's sword ripped across Aramis' neck and his head rolled to the ground. His body dropped to the ground, sword clattering at his still feet.

15

THE BONE QUEEN LUNGED forward toward Jackson. I slammed into her shoulder, knocking her off balance and directing the path of her sword to easily miss me before giving her a hard shove and knocking her backwards. She stumbled before catching her balance.

I ducked to the ground as the Bone Queen's sword rounded overhead, slicing through a few strands of my hair.

My hand grabbed onto Aramis' sword handle as I rolled across the ground, spinning back upright just in time to bring the sword up to block her next blow. Our swords slammed together in a flaring of metal burning across metal. She pushed forward, and I felt my arms starting to buckle under the pressure and unrelenting force.

Glancing behind me, I let my sword drop and pushed backwards. Her sword grazed my forearm, then hit the ground as I took the brief reprieve to get to my feet and a better stance.

She rounded on me, advancing with several quick thrusts that I parried away from and avoided her blade once again. She over swung and I took the chance to slash across her abdomen, clacking against several bones. I twisted my sword into her hollow rib cage and, using all my strength, pushed, sending her flying backwards, toppling to the ground and shattering the chain of the necklace. The gem clattered to the ground, rolling across the floor.

I advanced, sword up, and then brought it crashing down toward her neck, but she brought up her arm to block. My sword cracked through her bare bone arm and severed her forearm and hand from her body. They hit the ground and fell still until slowly dissolving into just a few old bone fragments.

She screamed and got back to her feet. In a rage, she lunged at me, swinging violently toward me, but I managed to easily dodge the ill-timed and poorly balanced attacks. We danced around the room as I began to attack back, cutting through the air until one blow hit hard enough to knock her down, sending her tumbling to the ground.

"It's over," I said. "This is where it ends."

She looked down at the ground and slowly put down her sword. As I reached toward it, I saw her move.

Her free hand scooped up the bones she'd lost and popped them into her mouth before grabbing her sword again and getting back to her feet. I watched in horror as the bones clattered through her rib cage and then bounced out the open bits of her body and hit the ground.

Grey smoke billowed from the bones and slowly human shapes began to form amidst the smoke and shadows. Two copies of the Bone Queen appeared out of the shadows. The three turned to grin at one another and then rushed me.

Blocking six hands and a sword put my body into overdrive as I stumbled backwards, struggling to block hit after hit that flew my way. Hands with bone tipped fingers clawed at my flesh, but I avoided the sword easily even as the bone hands grabbed at my arms, hair, and clothes.

Two arms wrapped around me and dragged me to the ground. Despite my struggling I felt myself fall onto the ground, prone and watching the shadow of the sword rise above my neck.

I tried to roll away but another of the cloned Bone Queens grabbed at my wrists and held me steady. I struggled as the blade over my neck raised and then started rushing toward me.

Instead of the brief flare of pain then nothing that I expected, instead I heard something slam into the bone queen holding the sword. There was an *oof* and then the distinct sound of two bodies hitting the floor and the blade hitting the ground. Jackson thudded to the floor beside me, rolling across the ground, struggling with one of the Bone Queen copies.

Taking the moment of distraction, I slammed my elbow into the face of the creature holding me down. It reeled backwards and another quick blow slamming the nose into the brain sent it stumbling into dust.

Jackson and another Bone Queen struggled on the floor, Jackson fighting wildly as clawed hands closed around her throat. She looked at me, then behind me. I turned just in time to avoid another copy swinging the sword toward where my head had just been.

Dropping low to the ground, I launched myself at the attacker. My shoulder slammed into the empty space beneath her rib cage and pushed forward into the empty cavern of her chest until it bumped into her spine. I pushed my shoulder and arm upward to rip through her rib cage, feeling the brittle bones give way under my touch. She screamed, then dropped into dust with the sword landing at my feet.

Grabbing her sword, I turned back to Jackson and her

struggle. Her eyes were wide, red rimmed and her skin turning ashen and grey around her throat as the Bone Queen's fingers ripped into her. Jackson grabbed at the necklace on the ground by her, and, with a last burst of strength, pushed it across the floor toward me. Then she fell silent and still.

The Bone Queen and I both lunged for the flickering gem on the ground, but I just barely grazed it first, pulling it from her touch and rolling back to my feet.

She lurched for me again, but I sidestepped and blocked her attack, slicing across her arm with her own sword. She howled and grabbed at my arm. Her skin had melted away and now only a blank skull with strands of black hair whipping wildly around it stared back at me.

I slammed her sword straight between her eyes, ripping through bone. A screaming wind tore through the chambers as her body dropped to the ground. I grabbed the second gem from the ground and pulled the sword free from the now totally still body of the Bone Queen before rushing for Jackson's side.

I shook her shoulder, but she didn't move.

"You have to finish it," Aramis' voice spoke up.

16

I JUMPED AND SPUN TOWARD Aramis' body, now sitting up, head attached and looking like nothing had happened.

"What?" I stared at him.

He tapped his chest. "So long as this gem is in me, I can't die." He let his fingers curl into his ribcage. "You need to destroy these gems before Renata wakes again. You've only stopped her momentarily."

Slow realization hit me. "You knew all along that stopping her meant you would have to die."

He smiled. "I've lived longer than I ever wanted to. I'm ready." His fingers curled around the gem in his chest. "Once I rip this out, you have to use her sword to destroy the rest of the gems. That will take care of everything. That's the only way."

I slowly nodded. "After all this, that ought to be easy."

He smiled. "Give me a good burial?" he asked.

"The best," I promised. "Thank you, Aramis."

He flashed a grin at me before closing his eyes. Taking a deep breath, he ripped the stone free from his body. Instantly, his skin melted away until nothing but a pile of bones remained, the skeletal hand still clutching at the stone.

I carefully pulled the stone from my friend's hand, and turned back to the still body of the Bone Queen.

She started to move and I knew time was nearly gone. I ripped the gem free from the golden necklace and placed it and the stone from Aramis over her throat and immediately slammed the sword through them and her.

Light ruptured from the inside out of the Bone Queen, ripping through her slowly, obliterating her skull then down her spine, and burning away every fragment of bone that it touched. As the light tore through her she lurched toward me, wrapping her hands around my throat. I coughed, pain searing through me and eating me up. Light flickered all around me until the flaring pain became overwhelming; everything went white hot and silent.

SOMETHING SLAMMED INTO MY chest.

A violent cough sent me doubling over, struggling with the weight over my chest. I groaned, "What the—"

"Don't you ever scare me like that again!" Jackson snapped overhead. "God, what were you doing?"

"Exactly what I told you I'd do, getting rid of the Bone Queen." I said, catching my breath.

"Yeah, well next time don't try to take yourself out doing it. I won't always be around to breathe life back into you, got it?" she ordered.

I smiled faintly. "Got it." I rubbed my head, looking around.

Only a few strands of dark hair and a small piece of metal from the hilt of the sword remained of the Bone Queen.

I turned toward Jackson. "You were dead."

Jackson blinked. "I came to and found you dead! I was just unconscious. What were you even thinking?" Jackson demanded.

I coughed and sat up, rubbing my chest, bruised ribs at least. "What do you think I was doing? Having a picnic with the Bone Queen? What did you expect me to do? I had to do what I had to do to make sure that she was stopped. All those gems are gone now, and according to what Aramis told us that means that she's gone, that she can't come back and do this anymore." I said, "That's worth any risk, even my own life."

Jackson frowned. "Well, regardless, I'm glad you're alright," she said, offering her hand and helping me get to my feet. "Now, if we're done, we still need to find a way out of here."

"First," I shakily got to my feet and found the collection of Aramis' bones, "help me collect these. Looks like we've got two funerals to put on."

Jackson looked over and bit at her lip. "That's Aramis, isn't it?"

I nodded silently.

She closed her eyes for a few seconds before joining me in collecting the bones and carefully putting them into her bag.

I groaned in pain at putting weight on my leg, but took a deep breath and pushed through it.

"This place looks well built, like the bottom of a building of some sort. I bet we can find a staircase or something. There has to be some way out of here and back to the surface. I'd kill for some fresh air." Jackson said.

Every part of my body felt tender and bruised. Hell, every part of me probably was bruised, but I felt somehow lighter. "She's gone. She's really gone." I shook my head, laughing. "You know, for a minute there, just a minute, I really thought she had me."

"I don't think anyone will ever really have you down for long," Jackson said, guiding me toward a hallway at the edge of the room.

"That's a lot more faith in me than you had when we first met," I said.

"Let's just say you're very persuasive after I've seen you in action," she said before she turned and took a quick walk around the wall. Pushing aside a few loose bricks, she called, "Hey, stairs leading upwards!"

"Told you." I tried to increase my walking pace to get to the stairs.

Jackson helped me, making sure I stayed upright in my haste to get up the stairs.

I stumbled a few times, but Jackson kept me from face planting and eating the clay. I grunted in pain as we climbed higher up the stairs and streaks of sunlight began to appear. The air warmed and suddenly wasn't so stale and coarse in my lungs. Against the burning pain of my injuries, I took a deep breath and then let it all out.

"God that feels good," I murmured.

Jackson nodded beside me, taking her own slow, deep breaths. She finally turned to me and asked, "What are we going to do about Aramis and Eten?"

I took a deep breath. "Well, we made a promise to them, right? We promised that we'd get a real burial site, some-where that Eten could rest in."

Jackson nodded. "I have a few friends at the funeral home here. I want to get him a real gravestone, something with his name on it. But, that's really all we know about him, isn't it? I don't even know what his last name was."

"Somehow I don't think that'd much matter. We've got enough. We can put them both to rest somewhere out here where they can watch over all this land and keep an eye on things if they want, but where no one will really bother them. No one except for us."

Jackson nodded. "I think they'd like that." She sighed.

"What about her?" She looked back over her shoulder. "Should we do anything with her?"

I shook my head adamantly. "She doesn't deserve anything after all the crap she's done. All she's going to get is buried down here forever. Soon as we get back to the surface I'm going to make sure every entrance into or out of the place is blown to kingdom come so nothing makes it out or back in. Whatever's down there is going to stay there."

Jackson nodded. "And I'll keep an eye on it, make sure nothing strange happens. And if it does, guess it's good to know I've got a friend I could call on for some help." She looked at me.

I smiled. "You got it. But first, I think a hospital visit might be in order."

Jackson nodded as we took stock of where we were. I slumped to the ground. Now that the adrenaline was fading from my blood, I could feel everything starting to drop and get heavy. Peering upwards, I could see Jackson waving her phone around for a signal and then I saw nothing but darkness as I faded out of consciousness.

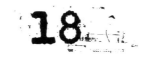

18.

CAME TO WITH JACKSON at my side, looking over my medical chart.

"You supposed to be reading that?" I asked, voice slurred with sleep.

Jackson jumped and dropped the chart. "You weren't supposed to be awake for another day."

"I don't follow rules very well." I winced as I sat up. "How long was I out for? When can I get out of here?"

"You've been here for two whole days. The doctors want to run a few more tests and keep you for observation. They're worried about—"

"Yeah, but that doesn't mean I have to stay." I pressed the nurse page button. "I know the leave hospital against medical advice forms well."

Jackson shook her head, smiling. "You get yourself signed out of here and I'll pick you up out front. I've got something I want to show you."

I nodded and watched Jackson leave just as the nurses came in and my next real fight began.

About thirty pieces of paper later, I was being wheeled to the front of the hospital. That was one fight I had lost; I had to be wheeled out of the hospital in a wheelchair. Jackson's truck sputtered up to the entryway and she hopped out to open up the passenger door for me.

I noticed my bike was pulled into the bed of the truck, all my things already packed. Just barely listening to the nurse's string of directions, I waved and hopped into Jackson's truck.

Jackson shook her head, waving to the nurse as the truck bucked to life and we sped off.

"You know you really ought to listen to medical advice," she told me.

"I'm whole and fine," I said, "and I've wasted more than enough time laying out in a bed. There's still all kinds of things out here that need my attention. The world's a mess, and I'm here to fix what I can."

She shook her head again and I winced as the truck bumped down the familiar road leading to the cemetery. I tensed for just a moment, and then relaxed. The Bone Queen was dead, and nothing dead would be coming after me anymore. Well, nothing sent from her at least.

Jackson parked in the gravel lot and stood close by as I got out of the car and hobbled after her. She led me into the cemetery, past the unmarked section.

"I had the entryways into those underground tunnels closed up," she said. "Real quiet. Don't think anyone but us even knows they're here at all."

"Thanks," I said, glancing toward the mausoleum we had originally entered the bone pit of hell through. I shook those thoughts away. "Where are we headed?"

"I thought you'd want to pay your respects," Jackson said.

I nodded. "You found a burial site?"

"Out of the way, but nice," she promised. "I think they'd like it."

She walked me past the edge of the unmarked graves and through a few sections of trees. Behind a rather thick growth of trees was a clearing where two very small gravestones rested side by side. One simply read 'Aramis' and the other 'Eten'.

I nodded. "I think you're right. They'd like it." I leaned against a tree at the edge of the clearing and closed my eyes for a moment. I wasn't the praying-all-the-time type, but for these two I sure hoped they finally found the rest they both had been looking for.

When I opened my eyes Jackson was watching me. "So, where are you going to now?" she asked.

I shrugged my shoulders. "Not sure yet. I guess home is a good place to start. I'm sure by the time I get back I'll have a dozen new jobs to pick up."

She nodded.

"What are you going to do?" I asked. "What happened with your job?"

She offered me a sly half-smile. "Well, turns out that a freak electrical fire destroyed a lot of the morgue. Several bodies were lost in the blaze."

"Oh? That so?" I asked innocently.

Jackson smiled, shaking her head. "I don't know how you do what you do. I don't think I ever could."

"I do what I do so that people like you don't have to," I explained, rolling my shoulders.

She nodded, and we stood in silence, looking over the gravestones for a few minutes before I turned back toward the cemetery. "Help me get my bike out of the truck?" I asked.

She nodded, and we walked back across the cemetery.

Working together, we freed my bike from the bed of the truck and onto the ground.

I offered Jackson my hand. "It's been a pleasure."

She smiled and took my hand firmly, giving it a solid shake. "It has been an honor, and if you ever find yourself in Epsilon again…"

"You'll be the first to know," I promised as I let go of her hand and climbed onto my bike.

The engine revved to life and Jackson waved me off.

Heading down the road, I put the Bone Queen out of my mind. She was gone, but there'll always be a need for the Pulptress.

ANDREA JUDY is a writer who makes her home in Atlanta, Ga. Passionate about language, she writes in multiple genres, and has had poems and short stories appear in various literary magazines as well as in several anthologies. She also studies and writes about fandom and video games.

27959374R00071

Made in the USA
Middletown, DE
27 December 2015